GOODBYE TO BOYHOOD

A COLLECTION OF STORIES

SPENCER THOMAS

BY SPENCER THOMAS LLC

Book design by Eva Polakovicova.
ISBN: 979-8-218-30668-7 (print book)
Published by "By Spencer Thomas LLC"
www.byspencerthomas.com

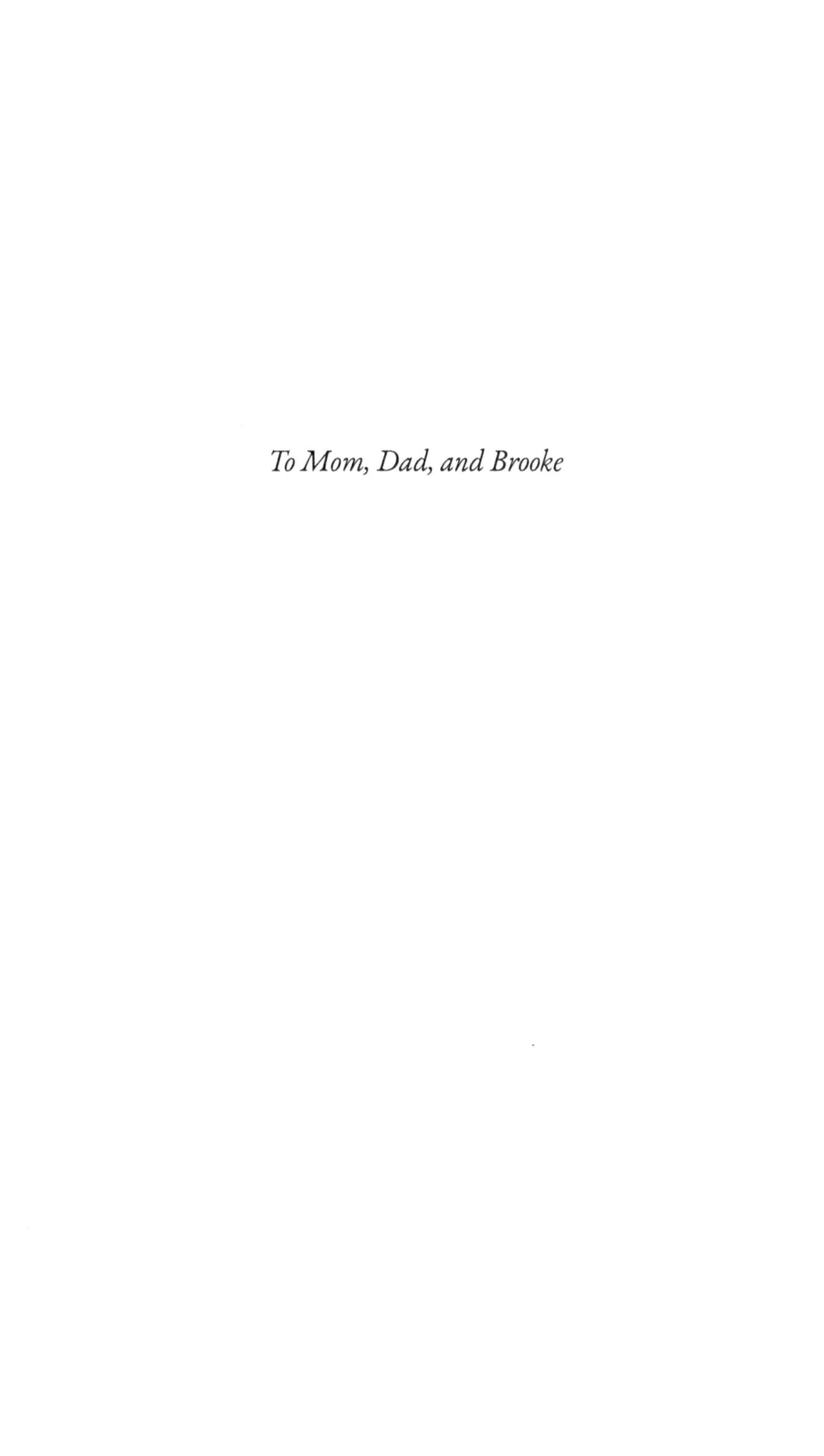

To Mom, Dad, and Brooke

PREFACE

When I was in high school, I tried to write my first book. I dubbed it *Unapologetically Me,* the epic tale of a boy who is, you guessed it, unapologetic. The novel, if anything, was a projection of my insecurities rather than an actual book with a plot. The plot was my own life, and the characters were the people I found within my own world: Mom, Dad, and my twin sister, Brooke.

I named the protagonist Hayden, and unlike me, he had friends. Where I was weak, Hayden was strong. Where I was always wrong, Hayden was always right. Where I was lonely, Hayden embraced his solitude. Hayden had it all. He was loved and became the version of the boy I wished to be. Despite the fact that I wrote a character so dissimilar to myself, we shared the same brain. And while my first novel never came to fruition, I felt less lonely writing about another boy in another world very similar to my own. At sixteen, I swore that one day I would write, finish, and publish a book.

So, at eighteen, I tried to write another book during

my freshman year of college. This one I titled *I Hate That This is The End,* and it was meant to be the tale of broken college lovers trying to forge a romance. The novel, in retrospect, was a fantasy. It was a byproduct of my venting. It was anger and sadness pooled into a collection of 130 pages—a declaration that the dreams of falling in love within a big city are all lies. Love is a farce and men only seek to betray. I was a teenager with aspirations of living in New York City, and once that dream came true, I was unsure of where to turn next.

Through trying and failing to write two novels, I told myself that perhaps it was time to step away from writing and be realistic. I changed my class schedule and began taking marketing classes, setting my sights towards another career. The life of a writer is a challenging one, and maybe I'm not meant for this life. Maybe I never was.

My saving grace came in the place where I always found clarity: English class. Tasked in my freshman year, spring semester with writing an essay on "modern love", my professor at the time, Timothy Tomlinson, had asked all of us to experiment with our pens. What *is* love these days? What does modern love look like? Inspired by Kristen Roupenian's *Cat Person,* the first line of *BOY* came to me on a winter night in February, 2022. "'Sex is purely transactional,' Boy says." I finished the story within half an hour, and soon, my first character came alive. A culmination of the worst traits found in a male culture of objectification, *BOY* became my new catharsis. Little did I know this would kick off two years of writing, editing, and re-writing to create my debut collection of stories.

Soon after, I found myself rummaging through my past. I wrote *Fathers* not long after, a narrative detailing the love between father and son—the battle between acceptance and adoration. While loosely inspired by my own life, the stories of *Goodbye To Boyhood* weave the best of fiction with reality.

I wrote *BOOBIES* during my sophomore year of college, a reflection on days spent in middle school trying to conform within a group of boys. I always felt like the outsider, and *BOOBIES* became my closure. I no longer have to conform. I no longer have to pretend I'm someone I'm not. I now have the privilege of friends who love and support me, and I will never take that for granted. *The King* came afterwards, but originally was titled *The Bully*.

Arguably one of the most, if not the most challenging story I've written, *The King* was a reckoning. How does self-awareness develop as we grow older? What's that specific feeling when someone takes your deepest insecurities and shoves them in your face? *The Bully* was set on a school field trip, but evolved into *The Unknown Word*, and finally *The King*. This tale is about building walls. Once someone tears through you, it becomes really easy to hide yourself away from the world. It's one of the many reasons I started writing.

Catharsis is always my resolution when I write. *Birthday Party* became my release, and I knew from its origins that it would later become the first story within this collection. It's a tale of isolation, but if anything, the entirety of *Goodbye to Boyhood* grapples with solitude. *Birthday Party* details the worst of loneliness but *Goodbye to Boyhood* (the story) demonstrates the best of it. Sometimes loneliness grants us a self-assured knowingness that we are enough.

The final stories of my collection came together in Fall, 2023. At the time, there were three different stories in place of *Boyfriends For The Night, My Mom's Boyfriends,* and *The TV Says the Moon is Going to be Red.* I knew these stories weren't going to make the final cut but I was panicking, trying to decipher what would take their places.

The first of the three final stories, *My Mom's Boyfriends,* was written in October. Furthered by the fact I was turning twenty-one that November, I kept asking myself questions. What does it feel like to grow up too fast? What pressures come with parenthood? Mothers and fathers are learning to live for the first time, too. Thus, I wrote *My Mom's Boyfriends* on an autumn evening, inspired by the collective narratives of others who have told me their stories. The first draft came to me within an hour.

The TV Says the Moon is Going to be Red came directly after. I always had the foundation of the story lingering in my mind, but by November, the idea clicked. The story was inspired by my own Grandma. I hope to make her proud.

The final story, *Boyfriends For The Night,* came to me as a passing thought a year ago. I even wrote another short story with a similar plot: *Discolight Fantasy.* You cannot venture out into the world without fear of failure.

This collection started with *BOY,* a tale of anguish and hookup culture, and was finished with me writing *Boyfriends For The Night,* a story of hope—a tale that proves love is out there and there is beauty in letting yourself be vulnerable, even when it leads to no destination.

Goodbye To Boyhood is the accumulation of trying to navigate the transition from the earliest stages of childhood into adulthood. One of the fears I had when writing these stories was age. I do not think that boyhood ends at eighteen. I am twenty-one, and still in a lot of ways, feel myself walking the line between adolescence and adulthood.

Boyhood is maturation. Boyhood is naivety, gained self-awareness, and growing. In talking with people of all ages across the world, it seems that boyhood, and the memories that stem from childhood, are always lingering. These memories will last forever, and set the framework for the future. Boyhood exists so long as you are learning and grappling with the transition between childhood and adulthood.

Thank you for taking the time to pick *Goodbye To Boyhood* off the shelves or purchase online. Maybe you found it tucked away on a library shelf. This is my debut collection—my first book ever. I welcome you into the world of *Goodbye To Boyhood.* You are always welcome here.

ACKNOWLEDGMENTS

My entire world shaped the makings of *Goodbye To Boyhood*, and there are endless people I want to thank, but no one more than my father.

There is, without a doubt, no one on this planet who has supported my love for writing like my father. Every story within *Goodbye To Boyhood* has been read, proofread, and analyzed by him in detail. The very origins of me writing stories started with my dad. To this day, every story I have ever written is immediately sent to him upon completion. Thank you, Dad, for pushing me forward on the path of writing *Goodbye To Boyhood* when everything felt so hopeless. You gave me courage when I needed it most, and this collection would not exist without your endless guidance and support.

The next person that I need to thank is my incredible mom, whose work ethic and drive have become part of my own. Growing up, I watched as she worked overtime in hospice care, taking care of dying people—putting others' lives before her own. My mother has taught me the act of selflessness like no other. She has taught me grace. Like my dad, I would not be here without the support of you, Mom. You have never shied away from encouraging my career, and when I told you I wanted to be a writer, you said 'go for it'. Your unwavering support, affirmations, and firm authenticity shaped me into who I am today. Thank you.

I also want to acknowledge the irony in *Goodbye To Boyhood* having a central focus on the relationships between boys, when the strongest, most powerful relationship of my orbit starts with my twin sister, Brooke. We share the same eyes and mannerisms, and as I get older, I have come to realize how much we have in common. My sister is the hardest worker I know, and her ability to persevere has inspired my own. Brooke is a warrior, a symbol of power and success in my own life narrative. There is no Spencer Thomas without Brooke Emiry. My sister is the foundation for my life, and I owe her my world.

I even recall the time when my grandmother picked us up after school and asked who our best friends were. Brooke, having always been popular, had a list of names written down in a green notebook. But upon asking me, I only had one name: yours. Such a sentiment has never changed, for you will always be my best friend. But upon acknowledging this memory, I need to give special thanks to the inspiration for the final story of *Goodbye To Boyhood,* my grandmother, Maga.

Please do not confuse my grandmother's name with he-who-shall-not-be-named. We claimed the name "Maga" first. When I was a toddler, my parents, for whatever reason, wanted us to call my grandmother by the French equivalent of her name, "Grand-mére". My sister and I failed at properly pronouncing such a name, and thus "Maga" was born. My grandmother, born in Flint, Michigan, was a teacher. I spent my days reading alongside her. We read everything together. Mark Twain, the Brothers Grimm, exotic tales from foreign lands. My grandmother also had endless stories of her own. My sister and I, day after day, hour after hour, year after year, would sit and listen to her talk endlessly. Her stories were elaborate and always ended with a loud belt of her midwestern laugh, and if I close my eyes, I can hear it now.

We lost Maga in August, 2022. I don't think my life, or my family's, will ever be the same. I wish my Maga could be here now to see that her grandson finally did it—he wrote a book. I am proud to be my grandmother's grandson, and I am proud that her legacy will live on in *The TV Says The Moon is Going to be Red.*

I cannot conclude my acknowledgements without thinking of those closest to me. My dearest friend, Senem, thank you for showing me true friendship. When I met you, life felt so lonely. You became my best friend and showed me I was worthy of love. You approached me during our middle school transition dance, shook my hand, and declared that we should be friends. You made me feel seen in a room where I felt like I didn't belong. You will always be my best friend—my sister.

Sophia, you never fail to make me laugh. Our memories together remind me of the movies, and you are my film reel. I love the moments we share together laughing about nonsense. I love your desire to explore the world. Thank you for helping me reach beyond my comfort zones. You have shown me that the world isn't so scary.

Thank you, Sarah Ruth and Erica for your friendship. Our laughs together have given me so much joy, and I love you both to the ends of this earth.

Finally, there is no *Goodbye To Boyhood* without the help of incredible editors and former teachers. Mrs. Wild, my high school English teacher, you changed my life. You showed me safety and gave me the chance to express myself during the awkward stages of being a teenager. Thank you for looking out for me and always having my back. Ms. Czel, my writing club advisor. You helped me create a world where writers would feel safe and encouraged. I always loved the conversations we shared together. You and Mrs. Wild were my safety net when I was discovering myself, and your support has led me here today.

Stacey Goitia, my editor, you helped me in the final stages to shape this collection into an actual book. You restored my faith and brought your expertise with you. This collection would not be complete without your magical touch. Thank you.

Eva Polakovicova, my cover designer. Thank you for bringing the world of *Goodbye To Boyhood* to life. You took the visions I scribbled down in sketchbooks and created a world of whimsy. They say to "never judge a book by its cover," but I'd be honored if someone judged my book by your cover.

I would also like to thank Taylor Swift. The album *reputation* changed my life and your voice has become my life's soundtrack, played while I wrote many of these stories. Thank you especially for writing *Clean* and the entirety of *evermore.* I'm a writer, in part, due to the inspiration you provided when I was a young boy in search of meaning.

Goodbye To Boyhood serves as a reminder to keep writing, to keep pushing forward, when everything seems doubtful. I now know who I am. When I finally reached the finish line, I only now realized that I've been Hayden all along. These stories have always lived within me, and now they are yours.

I am unapologetically me.

1

BIRTHDAY PARTY

In a blue world decorated by Mom and me, I sit from the sidelines and watch as my younger brother Jake is praised by the entire world for turning eleven. A party of more than thirty, the yard overflows with neighbors from across the block. It's a special blue world, extra blue, just for him.

Beneath blue lanterns, the yard reflects the shadows of every neighborhood kid, everyone I know from school, now scattered across my home. They weave through the trees and kick dirt in the air as they run. They all play together, and I sit and watch from the edge of the yard. I want to join in, too. Craving to be part of something, anything, I wish I could have someone's name to yell out, and they'd yell out mine back. But when Mom asked me if I wanted to invite any friends, I had no names to give her.

"Are you sure?" she asked. "Not a single person you wanna invite?"

"I have no one," I told her. "Jake has more friends than me."

Mom went quiet and pressed her lips tightly together. Devastation overcame her. Then, she pretended she never asked me the question at all.

The lawn chair is made of a brown wicker, so light it's practically bronze. The cushions are red and white, thinly striped, and worn at the ends. Eyesight cast towards the tips of branches, I stare from beneath the trees. High out of reach, Dad placed glow-up lanterns that flash blue, all for Jake. I can count them, one—two—three—four, and there's another light tucked behind a branch—five. The sky grows a darker shade of navy, with white clouds peppered through blue. The sky changes color for Jake, too.

A group runs past me again. A quick glimpse of purple, green, and yellow. I'm desperate to join in. "Hey," I shout out.

Two boys and a girl from across the yard turn around with flat faces, staring at me. It's the identical twins who live down the street—the Frazelli boys. They have brown hair and matching large heads with puffy cheeks and oversized ears, while the girl is a stranger. Her jeans drag against the dirtied grass, and her shirt is six shades of different purple stripes, matching her purple and white sneakers. They approach me reluctantly.

"What are you playing?" I ask.

"Oh, we're just—" the first brother starts. His shorts hang loosely over his knees and his face is thick and wide like a thumb. His lips barely move when he talks.

The other brother, with an even wider face, immediately taps at his shoulder.

"Nothing," he finishes.

I kick at the dirt patch beneath my feet. The grass is lifted from its roots and scuffs my sneakers. Incapable of looking in their eyes, I stare towards the woods. "You're not doing anything?"

"Nope." The second boy crosses his arms, swallowed whole by an oversized green jersey with a soccer ball placed on the center of his chest.

Tapping my foot, I watch the dust settle, mumbling nothing. "I understand," I finally say. The undertow pulls the group away.

"See you later," the girl in the purple says, looking back at me briefly. The three run away faster as they descend into the yard, clasping their hands together at some joke. I wish they would share the joke with me, too. But the joke may be about me. I'm not sure if I want to know.

Nighttime turns my world into even darker shades of blue, an entire sky glowing sapphire for my brother, while I lay in the brown wicker chair and question how I ended up here. My isolation turns to bitterness. Anger fills my head, and as I spin into the sky, I wonder how I'll ever have a life like his. How does my brother have it all?

The party turns bluer as the night fades away. Across the yard, another party unfolds. Mom and Dad entertain a circle of their closest neighborhood friends. It's mostly a combination of Jake's best friends and their parents, a new collective where they sit out on the back patio. The moms exchange loud laughs while the dads drink beer and talk about cigars. It's a simple life, easy to understand, and even easier to see how everyone came together: Jake.

Snot-nosed with fiercely-white blond hair, Jake has blue eyes of steel. His glare is always cold, and he never speaks to me much. He yells a lot, whether it be at a soccer game—he plays soccer—or when Mom and Dad don't pay attention to him. But to him, I'm his older brother, and I don't think he cares very much. I do.

When Mom asked me to help decorate the house for his party, I was already thinking about all the decorations we could buy. We wrote down a list, checked it three times—I'm very thorough—and went to the party store. Streamers of navy. Aquamarine lanterns. We even bought special blue forks, knives, and plates, all for Jake. I helped decorate a birthday party for which I never even received an invitation. He doesn't care, though, and that's okay. I'm meant to sit, and observe, and watch from the outside.

A flash of neon flickers again. It's Jake running past me with his entire friend group. "Jake?" I shout through the dark.

He spins around quickly. Heels digging into dirt, his friends fall in line like a pyramid behind him. There are the two brothers and the girl again, all pretending they can't see me. "Hey."

Jake, now drenched in sweat through his blue shirt, is out of breath. "Yeah," he mouths. He looks down at me, but I'm taller.

"What are you guys doing?"

"Oh." He looks back at his friends and then at me. "Nothin'."

"Looks like you guys are playing a game."

They start kicking at the dirt, too.

"Can I play?" I ask.

"Jake," one of the boys whispers through the dark.

My brother doesn't say anything.

"Can I join?" I repeat. "Please?"

He sighs out. "Fine."

I try to get closer to the group, but no one says anything. They all gather in a cluster, forming a circle, staring at each other and Jake. When they look in my direction, it's past me, as if I'm not there at all. Their nameless faces stare at me funny.

"So," I clap my hands together. "What's the game?"

"Well," Jake gasps for air. "It's pretty simple. We're gonna pick someone to be it, and everyone else hides. It's basically hide and go seek but in the dark and kinda like tag."

"Oh, we've played this before."

Jake turns his head away to the trees. He doesn't reply. "You guys ready?"

The group nods.

"Nicky, you wanna be it?"

The thick-headed boy with short arms and fat ankles steps forward through the group.

He gives Jake a fist bump, and Jake nods in return. His approval has been earned. A smile, barely able to remain hidden, spreads across the thick-headed boy's face. Everyone wants to please Jake. Everyone wants to be him, just not his brother.

Jake throws his fist into the air. He sets off his battle cry. "Count off."

"Thirty—twenty-nine—twenty-eight—twenty seven—twenty-six," the boy says, counting down. "Twenty-five..."

Everyone starts to run, scrambling in different directions throughout the yard.

I stare off towards the main porch and run to my secret spot underneath. Built like a little crawl space, it's the place where Mom and Dad store the hose and cushions during the winter. It's small, unnoticeable, and the best spot to hide. It's perfect.

Burying myself deep, I'm underneath the porch where all the adults are talking. I can hear their footsteps above, and I pretend to be asleep underneath our home. I count down the minutes now, lost in the conversations above.

"Oh, you know, Reed is such a bright boy," Mom says. Her voice is soft but her words are bold. Everything she says is with a firm knowingness. Mom, if anything, is always honest. "He's still figuring out what interests him. He likes to draw and read a lot. He's very creative."

"How's he with making friends?" a stranger asks.

"Well..." Mom's voice drifts off. "He's struggling with that. He just hasn't really found his pack like Jake has, but he will. It's just a little hard these days, you know."

"Oh, trust me, we've been there. We've all been there." The feminine voice swallows her words and follows them with a firm "mmhmm."

"Hey, Mom," Jake's voice cuts through the cracks of wood.

"Hey, honey," she says. "You having fun?"

"Yeah," he yells. His adrenaline consumes him, and a loud tapping bangs the bottom of the deck. Dirt that is stuck to the patio rattles dust across the ground and covers me in filth.

"Where's your brother?" Mom asks.

"I don't know." Jake yawns. "Haven't seen him in hours."

"Can you go look so we can do cake?" she asks.

"Do we have to—"

"Jake," Mom cuts him off. "He's your brother. Please go find him so we can celebrate your cake with him."

I can imagine my brother's look of disgust smattered across his face. His lips are probably caving in, and his eyes are narrowing. He's not getting what he wants. It never ends well. "I don't want to," he whines.

"Jake."

"Fine," he huffs, stomping around and down the patio stairs.

At first, Jake's words mean nothing to me. I continue to stare off into the darkness and imagine that I'm in a place where my brother loves me and where everyone else likes me. Then the truth shatters my illusions. *I haven't seen him in hours. Do we have to? I don't want to.*

I thought we were playing a game. I thought Jake was including me. I decorated his party in the hopes he would say 'thank you'. I did everything I was supposed to, and that still wasn't enough for him to want me here. I sink lower into the ground, covered in dirt and defeat. I'm nothing to my brother, just nothing. And I do not know why.

I slowly crawl out from under the patio in the dark, emerging from my tomb. My knees are covered in green, damp grass stains. There's dirt in my hair and across my shirt. Anger swallows me whole.

"I heard what you said," I yell at him. "Why don't you want me here? Why did you tell Mom you haven't seen me in hours when you just saw me?"

"Reed," Mom begins to yell.

I ignore her. I walk towards Jake until our eyes meet —a pair of brown eyes and blue with nothing in common. "Why do you hate me so much?"

Jake's friends gather round in a circle and watch like hunters, ready to rip me apart with mean words and a love for my brother, who doesn't understand how to love his own blood. Their parents start to stand slowly, drunkenly trying to navigate the patio and their children away from us fighting.

"What did I do wrong?"

"I don't hate you," Jake finally says. He looks me down and up again with disgust. His eyes tell me he disapproves of me. I sense he's disappointed to call me his brother. "I just think you're weird."

"I don't understand."

Jake goes quiet for a moment, unsure of what to say next. "It's not—"

"Just say it," I spit out. "Tell me why you hate me. Tell me why you hate your brother."

His face turns red. "Why can't you just act like a boy?" His mouth seems to explode all these words at once. "You are not like anybody I know. You are so weird. None of us are like you. None of us act like you. Don't you get it?"

I look down at the ground again. Both my feet, and even Jake's, tap against the worn out wood. Our mannerisms are the same, and yet, I'm the one who's different. Disappointment fills my belly and guilt builds in my chest. Jake doesn't hate me because I've done anything wrong—he just hates me.

"Just look at you." He laughs. "You cared so much about decorating the stupid party? Why? Only girls do that. You're kinda like a girl, always crying and complaining and being annoying. You don't even do sports. You're not like a boy at all." Jake steps away, avoiding eye contact. He quickly runs away. Mom stares at me in silence, and Dad ignores the situation completely. He's had too many beers. Again.

In silence, the pairs of parents, too drunk to understand what just occurred, go back to making small talk and pretend nothing happened. Blue and red beer cans are cracked open, couples fall back on striped cushions in wicker chairs, and everyone goes back to pretending.

We always pretend for Jake. He's allowed to make fun of me because he's Jake. Despite decorating this stupid party and trying and crying and trying to be enough for my brother, I'm still the bad guy. I'm the one everyone stares at like something is deeply wrong, and they're probably right, and I'm tired. I give up.

"Hey Reed, it's—" Mom starts to speak.

"No." I turn toward the house, walk inside, and slam the doors behind me. In fury, I scan across the empty, darkened kitchen. No one likes my streamers, so I'll help them out and tear them down.

I grab at my creations, ripping the blue up and tearing it to the floor. I pop the balloons with a knife and rip paper plates into two. I roll up balls of blue paper and toss blue cups to the ground, clearing off full counter-tops full of packed food, blue decorations, and then there it is—the cake. Jake doesn't deserve my kindness. He never did.

A bright, blue cake with the words "*Happy Birthday Jake*" is inscribed in white frosting. I know what must be done. With my hands balled into fists, I scoop out cake and smear out Jake's name with one swipe. I stuff my face full, imagining Jake's reaction to his destroyed birthday. If he thinks I'm weird, then I'll give him weird. If he thinks there's something wrong with me, I'll give him something to think there's something wrong. I smear the cake across the counters and stuff blue streamers into the cake's center, destroying it completely.

"Reed," Mom calls out my name, stumbling through the patio into the darkened kitchen. She flicks on the light switch. "What did you do?"

In the light, she can make out the details of her child who has failed to be a boy and is loathed by his own brother. I stand with cake covered across my palms, open shirt, icing dripping down my face, surrounded in a pile of destruction.

"Reed," she repeats, breath taken from her lungs. "What did you do?"

I smile at her wide. "Being the brother that Jake wants me to be."

"Go to your room right now," she screams. "What is wrong with you? Why would you do this? Oh my God." Mom grabs at her hair, unable to stay still, watching as I slowly leave the kitchen, covered in my mess.

I hold back tears past my fake smile. I'm deeply ashamed of who I've become. I wish to be like other boys, because then, maybe my brother would like me more.

I am completely alone.

2

FATHERS

I LOVE MY DAD. Isn't he just the coolest? He walks and talks and makes funny impressions with his voice. He can speak in a deep rasp that is surely scary if he wants it to be or in a high-pitched, mouse-like squeal. My dad works very hard and wakes up early every morning to head off to New York City. My dad's so smart—he's great with numbers.

My dad also loves my mom very much, and he's always placing flowers on the hood of her car and kissing her on the cheek, even if she doesn't want him to. My dad even lets me wear his ties, teaching me how to wear one myself. My dad is just the best.

"I love you," he tells me, as if it's in his nature to love me. My mom and sister don't have nicknames for me, but Dad does. "My Boy," he calls me. I'm his boy, and I am so lucky to call him Father.

At six years old, we watch movies together and fight with plastic lightsabers in my room. In the darkness, we fight back and forth under the glowing stars my dad hung on the ceiling. I jump to the floor, wielding my blue saber, ready to wage war to save the galaxy and defeat the Sith. With clashes and bangs, spinning and jumping, ducking and dodging, I avoid Dad's red sword as I stand my ground.

"I am the Sith," he shouts in a deep voice.

"And how dare you betray the force?" I shout back at him. Music plays out of a small speaker Dad bought because I asked him to, and as the tubas and trumpets and violins fire off in all directions, we fight as if the entire galaxy is on the line. I was born to be a Jedi.

Dad lowers his saber and falls to the ground in defeat, pretending to play dead for a minute, sticking his tongue out and spreading his arms wide across the blue and white carpet of my room. "Good game, Son."

"Thank you." I say. "So did I win?"

"Yes, you did." Dad nods. "Remember to be humble, though," he says as I cheer in circles around the room. "A winner doesn't need to brag about winning."

My dad always has the best advice. He's so wise.

———

As I wake up each morning and get ready for school, Dad sits in the kitchen and tells me about my future before I know what it even looks like. I'm now seven years old.

"You're so incredible, and your future's so bright," he says. "You will be anything you want to be, Son. You know that?"

"You really think that?"

"Think it?" Dad asks, scoffing at the word. "I know it. And on top of that, you're going to be big and strong and will fall in love with a beautiful girl and be happy."

After these morning conversations with Dad, I replay his words in my head. *You'll fall in love with a beautiful girl,* he says. *You'll be big and strong when you grow up,* he repeats. *You'll be happy.* I question if this is what I actually want, but Dad always knows what's best for me.

If I am going to be with a beautiful girl and that will make me happy, then that's the life for me. I take Dad's words as fact.

———

"You should do basketball and soccer, and maybe even baseball this upcoming Fall," Dad says.

We're sitting at the dinner table—me, Mom, Dad, and my sister Sophia, talking about our days. My sister is big into sports, and my Dad loves it. He wants me to play sports, too.

"He doesn't want to," Mom replies. Her fork bangs the metal bowl she eats a salad out of, while the rest of us eat chicken Dad made on the grill.

"It will be good for him, Em." My dad calls my Mom Em, short for Emma, even though she doesn't like the nickname very much. Mom prefers to be called Emma by Dad.

"Dave, he doesn't want to."

"How do you know?" Dad says back. "Let's ask him. Ben, do you wanna play sports?"

Now everyone at the table is staring at me. Sophia is

quiet, but her eyes are big and wide, just as Dad's are. Mom looks at me, raising her eyebrows, but there is no smile to be seen. She doesn't look happy.

"I mean," I pause. "Not really, but I'll do sports if you want me to."

"You will love it once you try it, and you'll make a ton of friends," Dad says, smiling as he bites through his chicken.

"But he doesn't want to," Mom says, speaking very fast. "Right, honey?" She turns to me again from across the table.

"No, but I'll do it."

"See, Em, he says he'll do it."

"*Emma,*" Mom's voice cuts through paper.

"Yeah," my sister Sophia cheers Dad on.

Mom goes silent, defeated, slowly eating away at the salad she made herself because Dad insisted we eat chicken for dinner. He always knows what's best. I don't know why Mom seems upset.

———

Mom sits silently on the side of the field as Dad yells out for me to run faster and kick the ball harder. I'm in my fourth game of soccer now and am almost eight years old. I started playing soccer a few weekends ago, meeting for team practice every Saturday and playing actual games on Sunday. When we do practice, the coaches yell at us and make us run between cones, kicking a ball.

"Come on, Ben," he screams. "Get the ball. Move. Move. Move!"

I can barely hear Dad from the field and my feet hurt in my shoes. There are even these pads covering my ankles and shins from getting kicked. Those things I like. The shin protector things are cool—soccer is not.

When we have free time from playing, I like to pretend I'm somewhere else. Sometimes, I'll act as if I'm in the mall getting my hair done, imagining someone's cutting my hair and making me extra pretty. Other times, I'll make believe I'm in some distant lands where there are dragons and pirates who can fly. I would be a hero there, a king even, and soccer would never be allowed. Ever.

But instead, I am on a field, running as hard as I can. Dad is always very happy when he comes to see my games and yells and screams and hoots when we score a goal. Mom doesn't say much.

We're in another game now, and this one, I really don't care about. As Mom and Dad watch, I only run through the cold grass so Dad keeps smiling at me. Mom will smile at me regardless, but I want to make sure Dad does, too. He tells me he's proud of me and thinks I'm going to be great, but will he still think the same way if I stop playing soccer?

I run faster at the thought, lunging for the ball, kicking it in front of my feet. I can hear my Dad yelling more now, screaming for me to keep running.

"Come on, Ben!" he yells. "Keep running, shoot into the goal."

I can barely hear him.

"Go right and then shoot!"

I keep running, and see a small boy with his hands out ready to catch the ball. Apparently, the goalie is the only person allowed to touch the ball with his hands.

I aim and shoot the ball towards the net with all my might, a good distance ahead of all the other boys from the other team, and even my own. The ball powers through the grass, but as soon as it gets close to the net, the goalie jumps and lands on it, stopping my shot. I can hear the other team yelling from across the field, but I don't look back yet. I don't want to see everyone's faces. I don't want to see Dad's face.

Defeated, I slowly turn around. I look up, and there's Dad from the end of the field, the smile wiped from his face. His arms are crossed. Mom smiles back at me. There must be something wrong with me for missing the shot. I hate disappointing Dad.

———

"I'm heading off to school," I shout from the bottom of the stairs.

"Have a good day, love you," Dad shouts back. I'm now older and a freshman in high school.

When I was younger, my father told me I could become anything I wanted when I grew up, but I would have to work for it. So now I work really hard and apply myself in everything possible just so I can make something of myself. I want to go to Harvard or Princeton or maybe even Yale. Not Cornell, though—it's too cold there. I stay up late after school for debate club and Euro

Challenge, where I pretend to care about the European Union's economic crises. I don't know what we're talking about—ever.

But when I go home, Dad is so proud of me. He's accepted that I may not be very good at sports, but I am good at something else: school.

He roots for me as I cry myself to sleep over passing Honors Biology and helps edit my English essays when I need a second pair of eyes to tell me what's right and wrong. He gives me the rundown on American economics, hoping it might help when I go to my clubs. He even gives me advice about life and the future. And girls.

"Women are so beautiful, and you'll be so lucky to have a wife and kids someday of your own," Dad says to me.

"Absolutely," I reply flatly.

When he talks, I listen and nod along. But the truth is, I don't care about women or getting married or even having kids because there's someone else. When Dad talks about girls, I imagine a boy in my math class.

His blond hair falls below his eyes, which are a bright blue, and he always wears clothes that are too baggy for his body. He's super smart and understands the complexities of math far better than I do. Everyone loves him, even though he's weird like me. He's been given such an exception for being weird. He's good at sports. Plus, he's really smart, and even won an award for being so smart— a scholarship from our high school to any college he wants when he starts applying three years from now.

He tells me about his older brothers and younger

sisters and how he loves Lacrosse but isn't tall enough for basketball like his brother. He talks about his father and how his dad named him after his grandfather, Noah.

In math class, Noah turns to me, extending his right hand, shaking mine as if we're about to conduct a business meeting. "Good day Ben, how are you doing today?" He speaks formally, as if introducing himself to me for the first time.

"Good day, Noah, I am good. How are you today?" I reply.

"Very well, myself. How are you?"

"You know, good, I guess. I can't complain."

"You excited for geometry today?" he says, still keeping up with the formalities.

"I must say that I am, in fact, excited for geometry today. I do love right triangles."

"I also, in fact, must admit, and say I love right triangles. A very astute observation, Ben."

"And very good manners to you, Noah."

We banter back and forth as if we're old Englishmen, and when the chatter grows awkward, we change the conversation back to our lives and our families and friends. He also likes girls, in particular a girl named Beth in our Spanish class he told me about once. I smiled and said he should go after what he seeks.

When I go home, Dad always asks me if there are any girls on my radar. He wants to know if there's anyone in school, any girl, I would want to date.

"You're fifteen years old, for God's Sake. Why don't you have a girlfriend, Ben?"

"How am I supposed to know?" I reply.

"It makes no sense—you're smart and good-looking. You should have girls all over you," Dad says. "Explain that to me."

I laugh at him in the doorway of his bedroom. "I don't know."

"Jesus fuck, Ben. You gotta be having fun, you're so young. When I was your age, I had my first girlfriend. Her name was Penny Cragan and she was French."

"Yes, Dad, I've heard the story."

"You get what I'm saying. Is there anyone you like at all? Anyone?"

"Nope, not at the moment."

"Well, let me know when you do and then we can strategize."

"Okay, whatever you say."

"I can be of help."

"I'll let you know if anything changes, but right now, I'm good. It's just me, myself, and I, and I'm okay with that."

"Okay," Dad says.

The conversation grows stale and the silence aches. "Okay." I turn around and walk back to my room, burying myself in regret. I wish he knew the truth. More so, I wish he would be okay with the truth.

———

I'M sixteen now and my Dad is still surprised I don't have a girlfriend.

"I don't understand what it is," Dad says. "Are you

gay or something?" He cracks a joke, as if it's unfathomable for me to be gay.

"No." I shake my head quickly, grabbing my hands in my lap, desperate for something to hold. I no longer have math class with Noah, but we do have Spanish together. We're seat partners. When we are tasked with assignments, we partner up like two people doing crime together, united by some common threat, both in search of an answer.

Noah is starting to fill his clothes in now. His shoulders are more broad, his back wider, his arms thicker. While I bury myself in hoodies, Noah's arms flex with biceps the size of tangerines. He's growing into a man, and I still feel like a boy. I dart my eyes away when he turns in my direction.

I'm scared I might break, nervous I might say something I would never say aloud to him—terrified I'll say something that my Father wouldn't support.

"I think I'm transferring schools," Noah says. It's the end of the day in Spring, and finals are around the corner. We're buried away in the back of the classroom corner, surrounded by white cinder blocks. The backs of our legs are pressed up against a metal furnace no longer in use, covered in crusted layers of white paint.

"Oh, really?" I say.

"Yeah, I think." Noah sighs, brushing his blond hair out of his eyes. "My dad really wants me to go to this school down in Virginia, which is really good for sports. It's private, so they would give me a scholarship, but I don't know."

"Why now?"

"For colleges, I guess," he says. "There's a better chance at me getting into a really good school there than here, especially for Lacrosse."

"Right." I reply. I try to keep my emotions veiled, my voice flat. I don't know how I feel. Or maybe I do and I'm upset. If Noah leaves, I'll never have a chance to tell him how I feel, not that I would anyway, but I would want the chance. Then again, maybe I'm not gay and this is confusion talking. Maybe my desperation for Noah isn't even mine at all.

"I don't know," he mutters. "I don't know."

"I gotcha." I go quiet. There is so much I want to say. I wish he could sit here next to me for hours, beside me in Spanish class, and he can tell me more about himself. I wish his kindness remained true and he liked me a little bit more, but my wish will remain a wish, buried in the corner. I beat myself up as I walk out of class.

The questions come at me in all directions, pounding through my head as I march through the doorway. Why won't you tell him you like him? Why do you feel this way?

You shouldn't feel this way. You are straight, you aren't gay. You aren't *this*. What would Dad think if he knew? Would he still love his little boy, the one who used to play lightsaber battles with him? Would I still be the same son who used to run around a soccer field, kicking a ball because he told me to, pretending to love my fate? Would he accept me? Would he even still love me?

———

"Love's a simple thing—" Dad starts to speak, prepared to give me another one of his speeches about love and growing up and himself.

"I need to talk to you about something," I say, cutting him off. We're sitting at the dinner table, our steaks lined against a white slab of ceramic on dark green placemats. The chairs are made of dark wood with intricate carvings around the back. The tile beneath my feet is square and yellow. I run my foot along the tile's seam as I dance around the truth.

"What's up?" Dad looks up from his dinner, taking another bite of steak, chewing it loudly with his mouth open. "Is it the steak? Do you not like it, is that why you're not eating?"

"No," I reply. "It's not the steak."

"So, what is it?" In between his words, he keeps chewing, taking heavy bites, and stuffing his mouth.

"I'm—" I almost stop myself from speaking, easily able to pretend that I forgot what I was going to say, and then we can brush off this conversation entirely. Dad would continue chewing his steak and I would go back to having more regrets, still unable to eat my dinner. "I'm gay."

Dad stops chewing.

"You are?" His eyes drop to the floor—his face goes flush.

"Yeah," I reply. "I think I am—no, I am gay."

Dad remains silent for a moment, looking back down at the table and toward the brown walls we painted together when I was a child, and finally, me. "Are you sure?"

"What do you mean, am I sure?"

"Well…" Dad places down his fork and knife, raising his hands to give another platitude. "Have you ever been with a guy?" he asks.

"What kind of question is that?"

"A valid one," he replies. "If you've never been with a guy, then how do you know you're gay?"

"I just do."

"Well, you gotta try something to know if you like it." He points at the steak. "I can say I like steak, but if I've never tried it, how would I know? What if I take a bite of it and once I do, I spit it out because I actually hate it?"

"But I am—"

"Maybe right now you think that you are, which is totally cool by me, but you gotta try something before you really like it," he says. "Do you get what I'm saying?"

"I do, but that's not how I feel. I've always been this way, I've always been gay."

"Well, I don't know, I'm just a little surprised. I mean, you played all these sports as a kid and were always seemingly into girls. I just don't understand—"

"That was all *your* doing, Dad. I never liked girls. I never liked sports. I never liked half the shit I did, but I did it for you. This is who I am and this is what I like. Do you support me?"

The silence in the room feels louder now. Dad and I sit and stare at each other, both quiet—both reflections of each other. He's ambitious and funny and strong, and I am, too. But we're also non-confrontational and peaceful. I don't want to fight with him, and he doesn't want to fight with me.

"Okay," he finally says.

"Okay as in what?"

"Okay as in I have nothing I can say here. You'll figure it out." He goes back to eating his steak.

"So do you support me?"

Dad raises his eyebrow.

"Do you?"

"I mean, it's the lifestyle you've chosen, so I don't see what I can do."

"It's not a fucking choice."

"Sorry, wrong wording. It's just not easy."

"I know," I say. I wish he knew how *this* was. I never asked to be like this. I never asked to be having this conversation at all. But here I am. Here we are. "But do you support me?"

"What is there to support?" He continues to chew his steak. "You're gay, it's just a sexuality. Why do you need support for that?"

He asks the question as if it's a no-brainer, like there's an obvious answer to this equation. "Okay, Dad," I mumble. "Okay." I get up from the table and slowly make my way to the sink to clean off my plate. The entire piece of steak sits untouched on ceramic. I dump it all in the trash.

"Don't forget to put it in the dishwasher," he says casually.

I take the plate and dutifully put it in the dishwasher.

I turn around and head upstairs. Dad continues to eat his steak.

————

I'M STARTING to think my Dad isn't always right and perhaps he has never been. Maybe he's not even the smartest, kindest, and most clever person in the room. I'm seventeen now, and Dad and I speak less and less and I stay at Mom's more and more. My parents are now divorced.

He is angry with me for my retaliation to his words. He thinks he's right.

"You're overreacting," he says on the phone. "Come home. I'm not trying to hurt you, I'm just being honest."

I don't care to hear what he has to say. His support matters more than some twisted, backhanded acceptance. His love, so long as it's surrounded by limitations, can only go so far. The ability for him to support me, who I am, who I love, who I want to be—that's the kind of love I seek from my father.

"Can you come stay the night and have dinner with me, please?" Dad calls me a week later. This time, I answer his call.

"Fine."

"Okay, great." His voice jumps at the sound of my acceptance, almost surprised I agreed to come over at all. "Can you take the bus here after school?"

"Sure."

"I love you—"

I hang up the call again before he can finish speaking.

"Thanks for coming." Dad opens his arms for a hug and embraces me. I let him hug me, but I don't hug him back.

"How's everything going?" I ask, as if my dad is some distant stranger I need to make small talk with in order to fill the silence.

"It could be better if I see you more."

"I wonder why."

"Can you just sit and let me talk, please?" Dad says.

"Fine."

I sit down at the same kitchen table I grew up with. It's the table where I celebrated birthdays, watched Mom and Dad celebrate their marriage, and where they told us their marriage was ending. It's the table where my sister found out she got accepted into college, and the one where I told my dad I was gay.

"Let me speak and then you can speak, okay?" Dad says.

"Fine."

"Benjamin, you are my son. I named you Benjamin because your name symbolizes strength. You are strong, far stronger than I was at your age. And because you're so strong, I neglected your feelings when we talked at this table last, and I am sorry."

"Is that all?" Part of me wants to continue to shut him out, to not let him in. Another part of me is desperate to yell out *I forgive you* because I miss my father. I miss my dad. But I remain stoic.

"I also wanted to say," Dad pauses. "That I support you no matter what."

"Really?"

"How could I not? You are my son. My Boy. And I'm sorry."

"Well," I choose my words carefully, unsure of how

to be vulnerable with my dad. "What changed? Last time I saw you, you said that there's nothing to support."

"I did." Dad's voice goes shaky. "I don't want to lose you. You're my boy and I am always proud of you. I don't ever want you to think otherwise, and I'm so sorry."

The roles have reversed. Now, for the first time, my dad tries to seek my approval. And while I don't know if his words ring true, at least my dad loves me. At least my dad *says* he supports me.

I get up from the table to give Dad a hug, leaning into his warmth. I wrap my arms around the man who raised me, around the man who taught me everything I know. He's no longer taller than me, and while his face is covered in scruff, he's balder now, with his eyebrows slowly graying at the ends. We share the same Roman nose and wide shoulders, traits passed down from my grandfather.

Time bears witness to whether his words will ring true, so I choose to forgive him. I merely hug him, immersed in the quiet calm of the kitchen.

"I forgive you," I immediately reply. "I love you." My words scatter in the thickness of his gray sweater.

"I love you, too," he says. "It takes a lot to be open like you were with me, and I dismissed it. And I'll always be sorry. *Always*."

For the first time in a long time, I can breathe. Life doesn't feel so loud.

"Thank you, Dad. Thank you."

Our tensions cool and we are now best friends again.

"Oh, by the way, not to change the subject or anything, but I got an A on my last biology test."

"You did?" Dad pulls away. A smile spreads wide across his face. "I knew you would ace it. Keep up the good work. You're killing it," he says. "Harvard is less than two years away."

I sigh a breath of relief. "I'll get there."

"You will." He says. "Just keep working for it, and you *will* get there. You'll be anything you want to be, so long as you put your mind to it."

"I will," I mumble. "I will."

For the rest of the night, Dad asks endless questions as we catch up on lost time. For dinner, he eats chicken, and I opt for a salad that I make myself. We laugh and chat for hours, and despite him now seeking my approval, I still find myself seeking his. But he supports me. What more can I ask for?

My dad is just the best.

3

THE KING

Around the river bend and past thick walls lies the castle. It's dusk now, and atop the hill, the final crumbs of sunset glow against silver stones. The view from the top of the castle extends beyond the horizon, past mountains and rivers and places where the boy dares to dream. It's a safe kingdom, with men constantly on guard around the perimeter, and more employed to defend the lands from neighboring powers.

Atop his metal and plastic throne, the king intently watches his kingdom. He's an honest boy, one beloved by his people for his earnestness. Everyone is accepted in the lands of Elementaria. The colors of the kingdom are gold and green, and the roads where the townspeople reside are lined with wood chips. The king knows the names of every member of his land, from the baker named Sue to the town's troubadour named Bill. And the king? They all call him King. He's a simple boy by simple means, and he's happy to hold the keys to his own kingdom. It's a safe place, the elements only controllable within these walls. Past them, the King would never dare venture. It's dangerous, forbidden territory.

But today, the King is alerted by his henchmen to a new threat: a boy lies outside the castle walls and is demanding to be let inside. The kingdom is under siege. "Quickly," the King calls out. "Everyone inside the bunker while I inspect the situation."

The foot soldiers march in a row to open the palace doors, while the King stands quickly from his throne before his men. "Let me do the talking. Stand down." They lower their pitchforks and knives, ready for attack. "Who goes there?" the King calls out.

"I wish to use the swings," the boy says. With a stout frame, brunette hair, and almond eyes the size of peas, the boy stares off into space while he speaks.

"The swings?" the King asks.

"Yes. I want to use the swings."

"Very well, then. You may enter my territory."

The King gives the cue to his men, who open the palace doors by pulling down on a large rope. The wooden door, a bright green, lowers to let the boy enter. In doing so, the kingdom disappears and the King, who is leader of a great land beyond comprehension, is back on the playground.

So it goes, the King is, in fact, not a king at all, but only a boy with a wild imagination and a desperation for a place to belong. The boy sits on the swings, perched at the edge of the school's lot, where he watches from a distance a world where other boys kick a soccer ball in an overgrown field, and the girls trade secrets on the monkey bars. Their ankles, licked by grass, are covered in dew, the ends of their pants stained brown from wet dirt. The boy and his land of swings exist in no man's land, where the boy is too much of a girl to play soccer with the other boys, but is too much of a boy to trade secrets with the girls. His existence lingers in the corner, where he swings away in silence, counting wood chips and creating fantasy worlds until it's time to go inside.

The boy, a quiet individual with a knack for kindness and a desire for friends, tries to befriend the intruder of his lands. Perhaps the pea-eyed, doughy boy is looking for a friend, too. But the stranger stares at the boy, and before he even has a chance to speak, the chubby boy murmurs a foreign word, *"Faggot."*

Taken aback, almost hurt by a word he does not understand, the boy speaks back to him. "Friend, what does that word mean?"

The boy does not initially reply. Instead, the two boys drift in opposite directions on the swings. He goes forward, the boy flies back. He soars toward the parking lot, while the boy flies backwards over the soccer fields where the game commences. "What does that word mean?" The boy shouts again.

"Honestly," the boy looks back and sighs, unaware of his own rudeness, and lets out a great yawn. "I do not know. I heard it from over there." His pudgy arms point left towards the fields. "Go ask him."

"Which boy?"

"That one," the stranger continues pointing. "The one in the white."

Far in the distance, past the kingdom walls, is a boy who sits on a worn wooden bench in white. He holds one of those green water bottles that all the cool kids have these days. It's bright red with the Gatorade logo.

"Thank you, friend," the benevolent King replies.

"We are not friends," the boy shouts back. His stout frame shakes the chains that hold the swing and he continues to drift back and forth, lost in his own world, ignorant to the boy's rule.

The King, now in contemplation, consults his counsel for advice. Back in his imagination, he sits on his throne at the end of a long table with a green tablecloth that has fringed gold ends. "My people," the King calls out. "I've gathered you here today to discuss a matter of great importance."

"Yes, my King," the great warrior recites. He's the head of the King's security and his most trusted advisor.

"We have had a visitor come with a message, and we must seek its origins."

"What is the message, sir?" Sue, the baker, says.

Several nods of approval and a chorus of chatter erupts across the room.

"Order," the King bangs his fist on the table. The King's confusion reverberates throughout the room. "As I was saying," the King continues. "A distant stranger came with the message that I am, in his words, a *faggot.*"

A gasp of horror fills the stone chambers. "What does it mean, Sir?" Sue asks.

"I do not know. Henceforth, I think I must go seek answers on an expedition."

"Why do you need to know the word's meaning, Sir?" The warrior asks. "Does it matter?"

The King goes silent at such a question. Why does he

need to know? What is the desperation to leave behind his walled paradise to seek answers for unresolved questions? Curiosity has always filled the boy's heart, and as King, he's always been determined to have all the answers. "I just need to know."

"So, what now?" a voice at the edge of the table asks.

"I journey alone. As all great kings must do, these are questions I need answers to. I expect all my people will be on their best behavior while I set off, and I promise to be back very soon."

The room goes silent. "Anything you do, my King, we shall support," Bill, the town troubadour says. Breaking out into song, he plays a melody while the King sits in silent contemplation. The song is soft, and Bill's voice belts a tune.

In search of new worlds,
the King must go,
hunting down distant foes,
searching and searching,
he must find,
answers that linger,
beyond his mind.

The troubadour's song is soon backed by one of the townspeople on the piano, and soon, the whole room bursts into excitement. *The King is off on an adventure,* they cheer. *The King is on a new journey. The King is leaving the kingdom to only return with a new abundance of knowledge.* The King applauds the efforts of his people and their support for his every move, and the next morning, leaves his chambers with bags packed, destination in sight: the boy in white past the river bend.

On a short trek from the swings to the edges of the soccer field, the boy's feet sink into the ground, the ends of his pants running soggy. The wind carries forth, and through the thick of the forest—bushes that separate the playground from the fields—the boy arrives to a new land. "Hello, friend," the boy says.

Standing next to a worn-out bench, the boy in white sits and collects his breath. Like a wise messenger, the boy in white squints his eyes and stares up towards the King in confusion.

"Yes?" he says through short breaths.

"I'm here from distant lands to ask you an important question."

"Huh?" the boy in white replies.

"I heard from that boy over there..." The King points back towards his kingdom where the pudgy boy with pea-sized eyes and fat hands sits on the swing set. "...of this new word."

"Well," the boy laughs. "What's the word?"

The King takes a breath, scared to even speak it. *"Faggot?"*

"Hmm," the boy rubs his chin. For being a wiseman, the boy in white does not seem very wise.

This might be a more difficult journey than antici-pated, the King concludes.

"I actually do not know," the boy finally says.

"But—"

"What I do know is that it's a very bad word, and that's why I said it."

The King's face turns white and fear pools at the bottom of his feet, planting him in the grass like he'll sink into the dirt and disappear out of sight. "Well, do you know who said it, and who does know the meaning of it?"

The boy in white laughs. "Take a wild guess who," he says. "There's only one person who would know such a word and who would tell all of us to start saying it."

"Who?" The King asks.

"C'mon. You're joking."

The King shakes his head.

"Jake."

The name sends chills down the King's back. He's heard rumors of Jake in the past. His town's messenger once told him that far past the river bend and beyond the mountains lies an evil king, far more cruel than the boy's own rule. Jake is a tyrant, someone so cruel that his townspeople crouch in fear when he walks.

Allegedly, according to another townsperson, he's a ruthless man who hits others when they do not do as he says. He's loveless, and according to legend, larger, faster, and stronger than the rest of the kingdoms and people combined. He's a winner, an Emperor at that, and compared to the King, the boy is a mere beggar in foreign lands.

"Thank you for the information, Friend," the King says, trembling as he begins to turn away.

"We are not friends," the boy in white interjects, offended the King would even suggest the concept of friendship.

Trekking to the kingdom where evil brews, the boy questions if he should turn back. Does he really want to know the meaning of this unknown word? Does he really need answers? Is the answer worth it? He could return home, stack his walls even higher, and be safe within the comfort of his own community. This could all go away, and he could pretend he never went on such a treacherous journey to begin with.

No, the boy tells himself. There is no king who lacks bravery, especially one who is determined to find answers. He needs to see this through. Walking directly from the fields to the basketball courts, walls of brick covered in graffiti act as kingdom walls. Unknown words are written throughout the enclosure, and screams grow louder as the boy approaches closer and closer.

In large clusters, these boys chase after a tennis ball like dogs. Madness ensues in this pocket of the school. Several boys shriek and run while even more wrestle for the ball to the amusement of the other boys. Their clothes are torn and scuffed. Their voices are dry from yelling. The courts are a dark place. An outsider, the King reluctantly walks until he reaches the edge of Jake's kingdom.

Dark storm clouds loom over the courts. Standing on swollen earth, the King is now just a boy, terrified and reluctant to enter a world where outlaws, thieves, and mischief are transactional. Be the King that you are, the boy tells himself. Be strong—be brave. The boy steps forward onto the pavement, and immediately knows Jake can sense his presence.

Like a pack of hyenas, the boys stop throwing the ball and all turn toward him, running on all fours, ready to rip the boy-king to shreds. Barking, howling, and twisting in their skin, they inspect the stranger—hatred foaming at their mouths. "Silence," comes a booming voice from across the courts.

Jake, with fiercely blond hair the color of snow, wears a shirt the color of blood. His trousers are made of blue denim, and his arms are much larger than the boy's. He's the size of an eighth grader, practically, a giant amidst a world of fifth graders. "Who do we have here?" Jake belts out. A roaring of hoots and murmurs surround the boy.

He swallows the spit built up in his throat and dares to speak. "I am here from a distant land in search of answers." The boy's voice roars back, like the King he believes himself to be.

Jake smiles at such confidence. It's a menacing smile, a pitiful one at that, but it's a smile, nonetheless. "Go on," Jake says. "That doesn't explain why you are here on my land, taking time away from my amusement."

"Well..." The boy quivers in his boots. "I was told from faraway lands that you know the meaning of this unknown word, and I would like to know what it means."

Jake laughs at such a question, rolling his eyes and stomping his shoes. "So what's the word? C'mon, spit it out." Colder than ice, Jake stares through the boy, restraining himself from telling him to run before he attacks out of sheer boredom.

"Faggot?"

The pack of hyenas start to laugh loudly, so loudly Jake himself cannot contain his men. "Silence," he screams out. "Silence, silence, silence." His voice commands the mountains and the winds, and even the storm clouds squeal at the sound of his voice. Even they are scared of Jake. "Why do you want to know so bad?"

"Well," the boy says, standing in silent contemplation. "I actually do not know. Someone called me that, and I want to know why."

"Ahh." Jake lets out a thick sigh, shooing his pack of followers to flock back to the court where they'll continue to play wall ball. "You're not going to like my answer." As he speaks slowly, he walks closer to the boy. Towering over him, Jake stands in isolation with the boy at the edge of his kingdom. The boy shakes at the sight of Jake's cold eyes. They see through him. They see the boy is no king at all and is just a pretender, just a sweet boy with dreams of being more than the manufactured outcast.

"Why not?" the boy asks.

Jake shoves him a little at the shoulders, sending the boy backwards. "Because *you* are a faggot." He laughs again, an evil laugh like the ones from the movies that scare the boy so much he has to pause the television. "I can just tell by looking at you."

"But..." The boy cowers in terror. "What does it mean?"

"It's actually pretty simple," Jake yawns through his resentment, calm and collected despite his cruelty. "It means to be a boy fucker—a pervert."

The boy shrugs his shoulders. "I don't know what that means."

Jake scoffs. "Are you slow or something? I'll make it simpler for you." He clears his throat. "You are a faggot—

a boy fucker. Instead of dating girls, you want to date boys."

"No, um, um but—" The boy stumbles over his words. "But I don't."

"Whatever you say, faggot." Jake laughs off the boy's existence. "Can you get out of here now? I'm a little busy."

Shoving the boy again, Jake pushes him off the courts and back onto the grass where he falls on his back. Jake doesn't even look at him as he turns away.

War has struck the kingdom. Wood chips fall from the sky as the townspeople go scrambling. There's so much fire. It burns through the grounds and trees that keep the people safe—that protect the King's people from faraway intruders. The moats go dry and the guards fall ill to some unknown fever. The kingdom is left with no defenses, nothing, except the King, who feels the weight of grief on his shoulders. And through the rubble, Jake walks through on his own, carrying a box of matches and crumbs of paper. It didn't take much for him to destroy the kingdom. He alone tore down these walls and scared away the townspeople. And now, what of the once legendary heroic King?

When the boy returns home, he finds all of his townspeople are gone. They are dead, washing in seas of blood with their mouths cast open, calling out to their King to save them, but he was nowhere to be found. A new feeling sits in the boy's chest, and it's not loneliness, it's shame.

It is the King's fault, isn't it? His curiosity had gotten the best of him. He wanted to know why the boy called him such a nasty word, and intuitively, he's always known why—because it's true.

A new wave of acceptance hits the boy: the life of a king is a dream—a faraway one, at that. So instead, all he can do is cry about it. But the boy knows better than to cry in front of anyone else, for that is not very man-like.

So the boy plasters on a fake smile, wipes away the tears on his cheeks, and begins to rebuild a new kingdom, piece by piece. Within these new lands, the walls are stacked even higher and thicker. His rule will be more cruel. He will not let any outsiders in, no matter how hard they try to enter. This new kingdom is on lockdown indefinitely and forever.

The boy will be safe within these new walls, trapped within a kingdom built of shame and terror. Spikes stick out from the tops of the stone facade and sunlight no longer shines from the early hours of morning until the late hours of dusk. It's a cold place, and the boy shivers in robes made of fur behind ice-lined doors. The King is back, but at what cost? He has his safety, but nothing else to show for it. To escape, he'll engulf himself in math, literature, and science, until he can go back and pretend again.

The loud chimes of an old-fashioned siren echo through the new, barren chambers and across the schoolyard.

Recess is over.

4

BOOBIES

There are five hours left in the day, forty minutes left in math class, and three boys beside me. We're in Algebra 1, sitting in the back of the classroom against a cinderblock wall while Ms. Puck—who we all secretly call Ms. Fuck because she kind of looks like butter—teaches us the Pythagorean Theorem.

"When we are trying to find C, what do we do with the legs of the right triangle?" Ms. Puck asks. Her hair is pulled back in a tight ponytail, her black clogs offering a constant state of clicking against the colored linoleum tiles.

Julia Thorpens, an eighth grader notorious for wanting to go to Harvard, raises her hand.

"Julia." Ms. Puck points.

"The answer is to square both our legs to find C squared, and then we find the square root of C, which in this problem is 12.5."

"Very good." Ms. Puck smiles.

The boys beside me roll their eyes. I sit in the farthest corner of the room, looking out past my alleged friends as she speaks. "And when we have the quiz, guys, make sure to write down the formula before you start, just so it's easier to remember, okay?"

A chorus of slight nods and mumbles is heard throughout the room.

"Oh, the fuckin' quiz," Josh Cartovas mutters. He elbows the boy beside him, Marty Watts, who nods along to Josh's words. He's Josh's sidekick, although neither of them would admit it.

There are two other boys at the table, Eric Sorkin and me. We've been a friend group since our formation in the seventh grade, coming to find each other in the cafeteria, morphing into a collage of desperate masculinity and body odor from not using enough deodorant before gym class.

"We need to study for it together," Eric whispers to me.

"Yeah, later tonight," I nod along.

I appreciate that Eric wants to study with me. Sometimes, I feel like a fraud with these boys—just another nameless face learning how to play the part, slowly coming to understand what it means to be a boy and how to do all the things a boy must do for their peers' approval. Ms. Puck stares towards the back of the room as she sees my lips moving. She doesn't say anything to me for speaking slightly too loud in class. I think she knows I'm playing the part, too.

"So, for the rest of class today, I want you to take

these practice problems and work in groups. You're going to be tasked with solving for *both* the legends and the C of the right triangle, and there will be some trick problems in there, too, so work together. Okay?"

Another chorus of slight nods and mumbles picks up throughout the room.

"Alright, guys, let's do this shit," Josh mutters. He turns around in his chair, staring around at the group.

Five feet and eleven inches tall but insistent that he's six-one, Josh transferred to our school last year from a neighboring town. He's overly transparent about the fact that he's had a harder life than all of us combined. Whenever he tells a story, he speaks of his old town as if it's not twenty minutes away, but rather exists hours away, a place foreign to our own understanding of rural Vermont. He carries a comb in his back pocket because he takes pride in his hair, although it's grown out to his neck and swoops in a bowl all the way down to his nose.

We pull our calculators out of our bags while Josh struggles to look through his backpack, constantly brushing his fingers through his hair as part of a calculated effort to fix his precious bangs.

"Josh, you look so fuckin' stupid," Marty says.

"You wish you looked this good, Marty," Josh says. "You wish." He emphasizes the word *wish,* genuine in his belief that all three of us want to look like him—we don't. He speaks as if spit will seethe out of his teeth, which sometimes, it does.

"Yeah, yeah," Marty replies.

I've known Marty Williams since the fourth grade when we both declared each other best friends. We were sitting in math class, similar to now, and Marty turned to his left and stared at me. "We should be friends," he simply said. I said yes, and our friendship blossomed. It felt good to have a best friend for the first time.

Marty wanted to be a lawyer, and I, a doctor. We made a good pair, and then Josh Cartova happened, bending Marty's will and resulting in the casualty of no longer having a number one best friend, because now my best friend is also Josh's.

While I talk, Marty thinks of all the things he plans to say to Josh. When I ask a question or tap on his shoulder, Marty will continue to talk to Josh as if I'm not even there. The video games they play together without inviting me to join in are a marker of their new friendship. Two friends on the hunt for survival in a zombie wasteland. Josh knows everything about games and girls, and Marty, while my best friend at one point, merely tolerates me now.

An awkward combination of tangled hair, thin lips, and pizza face, Marty wears red tracksuits to gym class and doesn't ever brush his teeth in the morning, leaving his breath to waft across the room, able to kill bugs if they get too close. He changes in the bathroom stall in the locker room, although who I am to judge because I do the same. I think he's so desperate for Josh's approval just because he wants to be like him.

"I'd rather kill myself than look like you," Marty says.

"Got 'em," Eric jumps in, clapping his hands together in hysterics. Only I remain silent, not because I want to, but because I do not know what to say.

"You, too, Eric, you're fuckin' ugly as shit," Josh declares.

"Not as ugly as Smith right here," Eric says, jabbing an elbow into my side. My stomach sinks into itself—I try to act unphased when Eric's elbow hits my skin. "Thanks, Eric." I fake a smile and roll my eyes.

"Anytime, Smithy."

The group has defaulted to a few different nicknames throughout the past year. Smith, short for my last name, Smith-Duncans, and from there, the names only diverge into fractions of real ones, nasty, short names that mean nothing. The worst of the bunch is—

"Yeah, you guys are all up my ass, but fuckin' Smithy has Play-Doh face. How can I look worse than that?" Josh says, his laugh full of phlegm and gurgling out the sides of his mouth.

"Shut up." I can't hide my demeanor when they call me such a nickname.

There it is: Play-Doh Face.

The name Play-Doh Face originated after a rough gym class, when outdoor Capture the Flag turned into a fight for status and approval from boys more popular than me. I ran, sprinted, dodged, ducked, and threw balls under a scorching sun, and by the end of class, Eric recounted that my bright red, puedgy cheeks resembled the red Play-Doh he used to play with as a child.

Now, I'm known as Play-Doh Face, a name I accept at face value but sometimes cry about. I do not want to be their Play-Doh—a product of whatever they want me to be. They mold me like red rubber with a deviant will, but if I stand up for myself, they'll leave me. Being Play-Doh face is acceptance. Being Play-Doh face allows me the chance to have friends.

Whenever I sweat or my cheeks turn red, the group all turns to me and yells my nickname. One time, Josh even tried to grab my cheeks to stretch them. I merely turned the other way and laughed it off.

"Let's just do our work, okay, boys?" Marty now deflects the conversation, protecting me from Josh's wrath and Eric's antics, probably because he feels guilty for dropping me as his best friend.

"Where do we start?" Eric asks. "I wasn't listening to her."

"With the questions, dumb fuck," Marty says.

"Don't be a dumb fuck—we literally are just solving for each side, Eric," I chime in.

"Okay, so let's do it. Question One." Marty tries to steer the conversation now.

We sit in silence for a minute reading over the worksheet, four pieces of paper stapled together with various pictures of triangles of different sizes. There's even a square broken off into two right triangles.

"Hey, Smithy." Eric nudges me again. "Look at my calculator," Eric lets out a small giggle.

With thick eyebrows that connect in a deep unibrow and tamed black hair, unlike Marty's, Eric prides himself on being the prized child of two middle-aged doctors, anesthesiologists, who, as he told each of us individually and together, make a combined income of over a million dollars.

He loves being rich almost as much as he finds comfort in his cruelty. There he sits at the cafeteria table, berating each of us, making us tokens of his jokes and sick pranks, and when he goes home, he lies in his bed and finds euphoria in all the ways he hurt someone earlier that day.

I hate him, but I still find myself falling back on him for weekly calls and debriefs of the previous day, delving into math homework and all the ways Marty is obsessed with Josh.

"Smithy, you there?" Eric asks. "Earth to Smithy. Look." Turning the calculator towards me, written in numerical sequence are the numbers *5318008*.

"What is it?"

"Turn the calculator upside down."

"Okay." I take the calculator from Marty's hand, flipping it in my hands. Written in digital letters is the word "*boobies*" in all capitals.

"That's it?" I force a laugh through my gritted teeth, swallowing my shame as I smile back at Eric.

"It's so good," he says. "You can do more words, too. Lemme see it."

Eric takes it back, rewriting a new word. *boob*, *boobs*, and back to *boobies*. "'Boobies' is my favorite one on the calculator," Eric says.

I laugh forcefully, but no one ever questions my inauthenticity.

"Do it on yours," he says.

"What are you two doing?" Josh asks, looking up from a separate conversation he's having with Marty.

"Smithy is gonna write something on the calculator to show you both. Right, Smithy?"

The three of them stare at me, waiting for me to reply. Part of me wants to say no because I want to have my own say in life and don't want to do anything they tell me. But another part of me is saying I'm being irrational.

As a boy, you must never say no to the will of the friend group. Your opinion is the group's opinion. This is what friend groups do. They joke with each other and pick one another apart and write the word *boobies* on a calculator. Eric is cruel because that is how we operate, and thus, like everyone else, he's normal. Marty and Josh are best friends and I'm their friend, too, and this isn't some competition. I'm being dramatic. Like Play-Doh, I'm wrapping myself in a tight ball and need to unwind myself.

"Too much Play-Doh in those ears," Josh sneers. "Show us the calculator."

Staring at the black and navy board, I write the numbers *5318008* and flip it upside down, pushing my calculator across the desks towards Marty and Josh.

"Anyway…" I let the calculator do the speaking, playing into the jovial nonsense of boyhood because I'm desperate for their approval.

Josh bursts out with his obnoxious laugh, spit flying out of his mouth. Marty examines the calculator, and after watching Josh break out into laughter, follows suit.

"This is the great message you had to share with us, Smithy?" Josh looks at me with intent now, as if I have served my purpose well. His green eyes pierce through me. He knows what to say to break me. I play along with his games.

Slowly, I find the more I play the role as Play-Doh face, the more I realize maybe the role isn't worth it. "Yeah." I nod along, shrugging my shoulders, aware of the fact I am only a character.

"Good shit, Smithy. Respect it." He shoots me a fist across a table, a sign of approval—I did good. I made it another day in the group. I can breathe.

"Let me see the calculator again," Eric says.

I hand it over.

"Oh, Ms. Puck?" Eric raises his hand.

"Eric, what are you doing?" Marty asks.

Eric laughs and looks away.

"Give me that." I try to take the calculator back, but Eric giggles manically and holds it out from the other end of the table.

Josh says nothing now.

"Eric, stop, don't do that," I repeat.

Marty's face turns red as he tries to snatch the calculator from Eric. "Give it to me."

Eric pulls it away, wielding it in his arm. "C'mon Marty," he snorts. "It's just a joke. Play along."

"Stop it, Eric." Marty lunges for the calculator across the table as Eric pulls away. "Seriously, don't do that to Smithy."

"Do what?" Eric shrugs his shoulders, giggling a little more, ready to take his antics too far, just so he can feel better later when he's home alone and his parents are at the hospital.

Before any of us can say anything more, Ms. Puck

approaches the table, a mere clog step away from peering over the four of us. "Yes, boys?" She stands before us now, tapping her clogs on the classroom floor, a symbol of power. I don't want Ms. Puck to hate me for writing *boobies* on the calculator. I don't have the same opinion as the rest of the group. I'm *not* one of them.

"Are you boys lost on the practice problems?" Ms. Puck asks. "I can help."

"Yeah, we need help, especially Smithy here." Eric sneers his words, relishing his rage.

"Okay, what do you need help with, Jamie?"

"Oh, um, nothing, I'm good, I don't need help at all."

"But he does, Ms. Puck." Eric hoots and smiles through his twisted lips. "You see, his calculator answers are off. Show her, Smithy."

Eric slides my calculator across the desks, facing upside with the word *boobies* scribbled in its confines for Ms. Puck to see.

"What is that?" Ms. Puck asks, pointing towards the calculator facing her desk.

"What's what?" I can feel my face flush, the embarrassment riding in.

"Jamie, what does the calculator say?" Ms. Puck repeats herself.

"I don't know." The table goes silent, the rest of the class starting to cock their heads towards us.

"Let me see it." Ms. Puck snatches the calculator and flips it upside down, inspecting the word *boobies* written for her to see. Somehow, her ponytail is even tighter than before, her lips even more thin. She looks down at me and shakes her head, sighing. "This is not the assignment."

I remain quiet. Looking across the room, Marty holds his head down—he feels guilty, too. Josh bites at his lip, fidgeting with the dirt hidden under his fingernails. And to my left, Eric fights back laughter, his cheeks full of hot air—red and ugly and full of contentment.

I don't want her to think I'm like *them*. But maybe I am. My desperation makes me an integer—a whole number blending in with the digits around me until I lose any part of myself that is inherently mine. I'm the summary of added parts, so hopeful to feel part of a group, scared to remain a fraction, I lose myself completely.

Ms. Puck turns around with my calculator, facing the entire room.

"Class," she says flatly, her one word carrying its way across the room like the parting of the seas. Everyone's eyes are on Ms. Puck and on the little dot behind the film screen: me.

"Please make sure we remain focused on the assignment on hand and don't get distracted—" She waves my calculator around in the air. "—by typing profane words into your calculators."

She places my calculator on the table and stomps her way back to the front of the room, while the rest of the class remains in awe. I can feel the eyes of every eighth grader on my back—some giggling, some rolling their eyes, some confused.

"Oh, that was so good," Eric says, hooting out another choked laugh.

Marty and Josh become inaudible. They do not speak a word.

"You completely fucked me over, dude," I say. "Why did you do that? That was so uncool, what the fuck?"

"Are you serious, Jamie?" Eric scoffs, shrugging his shoulders like his actions do not matter—like my anger isn't important enough for him to care. "What's the matter, it was funny. Don't do dumb shit next time."

"It was your doing, not mine."

"Whatever you say." Eric rolls his eyes as if I'm being overdramatic, which maybe I am, I don't know. "Marty?" Eric asks. "Josh?"

I look at both of them, staring down at Marty. I want him to take my side, to stand up for me. I want him to say something, anything.

"Let's just move on, okay?" Marty says.

Josh nods along.

"Yeah." The group, for the first time in history, looks at the math papers and actually starts working through the practice set. My feelings are ignored, and Eric is vindicated.

What Josh thinks is what the group thinks. What Eric does is what the group does. Even what Marty has to contribute becomes a subject of the group. My existence, my own choices in the matter, become one with the group. Because Eric thought his stunt was funny, now the rest of us think the stunt is funny. I go mute, and nod along to the will of my friends.

I've lost again.

———

THERE ARE four hours left in the day, forty minutes left in math class, and no more boys left besides me. I'm older now and many years have passed since eighth grade.

I haven't seen Marty, Josh, or Eric in years. The last I heard of them, Josh came out as gay and Marty got a girlfriend. Eric attends UNC Chapel Hill like his parents before him. The last I heard from them was when Josh texted me out of the blue a few summers back, asking, "How are you?" Maybe he heard that I had come out as gay, too, or maybe he wanted to catch up like we were best friends who had something in common. I never texted back. I think I might've even deleted the message entirely. But even so, I can still picture each of them now, after all these years, standing before me.

There's the Eric I once knew in middle school, a distorted memory of curly hair with a freckled face mouthing out the words "Play-Doh Face" across the lunch table. His thick eyebrows raised and lowered with the words he slowly spelled out for me to hear over and over again. I imagine he's grown out his black hair. Allegedly, he got super into bodybuilding and has stretch marks running across his shoulders from all the heavy lifting. I wish him well.

I wonder if Marty still wears his favorite red track-suits. Would the boy I considered my best friend forever now apologize?

Does Josh still carry his hair comb in his back pocket? Did he ever move back to the hometown he loved so much, where his dad worked at a restaurant and his mother spent all her time at the general store? And what do they think of me, if they even have a passing thought about me at all?

I don't know if they do, but I know I still think about them. I don't know why, but I do. Do they ever remember eighth grade math class and say my name aloud, Jamie Smith-Duncans, and ask themselves *Whatever happened to Jamie? Whatever happened to Play-Doh Face?* Do they remember the time I got yelled at for typing *boobies* into the calculator, and how we used to call Ms. Puck, Ms. Fuck? I'm sure they still laugh at that one if they do.

But what I want to know most now is if they're sorry. You can seal doors and chart new territories, but you might never find closure. Do they know I manufactured myself into a product of their creation? I picked myself apart, rolled myself around on the countertop, and molded myself like the Play-Doh they saw me as. And even after all my transformations, all my new designs and shapes and colors, I still wasn't enough.

Now a sophomore in college, I sit in statistics class, a course I need to take to graduate. Alongside me sits my best friend, Sarah. She insists everyone call her by both her first and middle name—Sarah Ruth. She's from the south and has thick, red lips and rosy cheeks. Her smile is true, and unlike my friends from years before, she is kind to everyone, especially me.

We sit in the back of the classroom, whispering to each other while trying to make sense of the constant influx of questions and problems sets that look like a foreign language. Using the same calculator from eighth grade, I type various words into it out of boredom. A random surge of impulsivity comes over me. *5318008.* I type out the number sequence.

Sarah Ruth watches from my right as I fidget with the calculator, her fluffy, brown hair bouncing over her shoulders as she tries to peer over my desk. She sits cross-legged and adorns a pair of skin-tight dark jeans paired with a light blue sweater. "What are you writing?"

With a grin smeared across my face, I keep my eyes planted towards the calculator. "Flip the calculator upside down."

Red nails to silver plastic, Sarah Ruth takes the calculator from my desk, and flips it. She cracks a smile and shakes her head in disbelief. "You wrote *boobies*?"

Through a bitten lip, I laugh. "Perhaps."

"That's the important message you were writing down?" Sarah Ruth lets out another giggle.

Her laugh is contagious, and as she giggles, I try to hold myself back from an outburst. "Yup," I casually reply, clamping down on my lip with gritted teeth.

"How original." She shoots me a grin, and we lock eyes. "In statistics class, of all places." She slaps her hands to her face as if I committed a grave atrocity. "Good grief," she whispers, as if she's a southern woman shocked at the horrors of writing the word *boobies* in the calculator.

Following suit, I slap my hands on my face in horror back. "I know, right? How dare I?"

We both nudge at each other and for the remainder of class, mumble about anything that isn't statistics.

At the end of the hour, I take one final look at the untouched calculator. The word *boobies* is still written across its body, the word a mere series of numbers combined and flipped upside down. What was once conformity is now freedom of expression.

With no hesitation, I erase the typed-out *5318008*, wipe the calculator clean, and turn towards Sarah Ruth, who cracks another joke. Then I laugh, too.

5

MY MOM'S BOYFRIENDS

I STARE at my mother within the stars. She holds me like Venus and cradles me while I wander lost, somewhere in between Mars and Saturn. "Mommy," I call out to her. Her embrace is greater than the universe, and we travel through space together. A little light projector whirs in the corner, working at light speed, trying to pump a universe atop my ceiling.

Her voice is the galaxy, so soft and omnipresent, she rules all. God is even carried away by her charm. "How much do you love me?" I ask. I already know the answer, but I love hearing Mommy tell me again and again. She cannot sing, but her voice is so soft, so familiar. I hold onto her words because that is all I know to be true.

"My love," she coos. Mommy wraps her arm around me, but I can't feel her skin. She's wrapped in thick pajamas—black cotton. "I love you more than this entire universe." She points towards the ceiling with her other arm pressed to my ear.

"Really?" I speak with uncertainty, just so I can hear her love me again.

"You bet, really." She giggles, but it's a faint whisper. Mom is like space, so emotive yet impossible to truly understand. She's quietly emotional, letting out a smile but never a laugh. Letting out a cry but never a reason why she's so upset. But tonight, my mother is happy and she loves me so much.

"More than the entire universe and all the stars across the ceiling," she continues.

"What about that one?" I point towards a large, green dot spinning in circles in the center of my ceiling.

"Even more than that one," she reassures me.

"What about that one?" I point to another green star, barreling past the first one.

"More than all of the stars combined." She squeezes me nice and tight. "Really."

I let myself rest as she speaks. My arms go limp, and my face softens atop her chest. Collarbone and soft skin serve their purpose.

Space is so beautiful. It's quiet here—endless. Green dots dance and move across the universe, and I fly through distant time and endless hours. My mom's voice is fainter now, farther away. Earth and Mars disappear into the distance, simply dots in the dark. Bright lights up ahead. It's Jupiter and Saturn. I dance along Saturn's ring as I continue towards Neptune, where I'll ascend farther and farther. I'm past space and I'm leaving the Milky Way. I'm safe here—untouchable.

"Leave." A booming voice interrupts my universe. Perhaps it's a misunderstanding. I continue my journey, but even louder now, "Leave." The shouts of a deep voice contort quickly. It's the voice of my mother screaming. "Get out, get out, get out." She repeats in cries. Awake now, space is gone. My room is dark, and I'm no longer untouchable.

Slinking out of bed, I creep up to my door, tiptoeing. Mommy cannot hear me. She mustn't know I'm listening. The hallway that leads to Mommy's room is a rough, sandy carpet with little square boxes. I step in each box one at a time, slow and steady, careful. Mom, like space, can see all. I need to be invisible.

"You need to leave right now." Mom's voice rises, beating against the walls of our home. My two sisters, one two years older than me and one two years younger, hide in their rooms. Whenever there's yelling, I'm the one who's always in charge of investigation.

"I am not leaving."

"If you do not leave, I am going to call the cops—"

"Do not do that, listen to me." The voice pleads, screaming practically for my mother to listen. "Just let me explain myself."

"What explaining is there left to do?" Her voice is harsh. Like rain, sharper, even. It's acidic. Asteroids tearing through planets. Moons crashing into other moons. She's on fire. "Leave my house."

Footsteps follow quickly. I turn to run, clambering across little squares to my room, but it's too late. Mommy opens the door, my back to her fire.

"Ozzy," she mutters.

I do not dare look at her.

"Your room. Now."

I run quickly and shut my door while their yelling continues. I try to focus on space, but even the stars cannot distract me now. Her love feels cold and our house feels broken. I pray for quiet while the yelling continues for hours more until I eventually fall asleep from exhaustion. I'm ten years old and this is my Mommy's first boyfriend after leaving Daddy.

I no longer call my parents Mommy and Daddy anymore.

———

Mom's first boyfriend after her divorce started with Samuel. They met through mutual friends, and Samuel told Mom she was the most beautiful girl he had ever seen past the age of forty. He works in construction and inherited a company that belonged to his father. He drives a large, white SUV that's very clean, and tapes a picture of our mother on the inside of his car's dashboard mirror. My older sister Vanessa doesn't trust him. "He's a cheater," she says.

We sit in the car while Mom waits for our coffees inside Dunkin' Donuts. It's been a daily school tradition while on the drive to school, Mom will stop and grab Dunkin'. A chocolate glazed donut for me and a medium iced latte, Mom allows me to get coffee on condition that it's "kid's coffee—" mostly sugar, vanilla, milk, and only a little caffeine.

"I'm sure he's very nice if Mom chose him," my sister Bridget says.

"No." Vanessa cuts through her words. "Then why was there all that screaming again last night?"

I yawn at Vanessa's antics, shrugging my shoulders. "This has been going on for two whole years. They always fight like that. Nothing is new. I'm sure it's just one of their fights—"

"Another fight because he cheated on her." Vanessa smacks her hand against the leather car seat. "Again."

"Maybe," I shrug. "But what exactly can we do?"

"Hush up, she's coming," Vanessa barks at me quickly.

"Hello my children," Mom says.

We chant back in unison. "Hi, Mom."

She wears a pair of thick, black sunglasses and stares forward out the car window. "What are you three talking about?" Her question, while naive in nature, comes with complexity. She wants to know what we are saying about *her,* and like God, my mother knows all.

Vanessa dares to speak first. "About you, actually."

"Oh." Mom cocks her head to her shoulder. "Is that so?"

"Yeah," Vanessa says flatly. "We were just curious why there was so much yelling coming from your room last night. Again."

"Well, you know." Mom pauses, taking a sip from her large, iced vanilla latte with skim milk. "I was just having a conversation with Samuel and it got a little heated."

Vanessa rolls her eyes, and I watch the two of them gear up for another fickle argument. "Only a little?"

"Yes." Mom bites her lip through the plastic straw. "Only a little. It happens."

"Right." Vanessa goes silent.

Laughing, Bridget and I stare across from each other. The car ride from Dunkin' to school is silent before the explosions. It's only a matter of time until—

"What do you mean by that?" *Boom.*

"I just think it's a little insane you're still with a man who cheats on you." Vanessa goes in for the kill, shooting off bullets to pierce through the skin.

"Maybe you should be focusing on yourself, especially those grades of yours, before you come for me," Mom fires back, deflecting Vanessa's ammunition. "I am young and in a relationship and we are very perfectly happy. There is no cheating going on."

"Then what was last night—"

"Shut it." Mom uses her powers to shake the earth and rattle the car. "It is *none* of your business. We are very happy together, and you'll see Samuel very soon."

Throwing her fist into the air, Bridget starts chanting. "Fight, fight, fight, fight—"

"Shut up" Vanessa yells back.

"Enough, Bridget." Mom sneers.

And just like that, Mom and Vanessa are best friends again.

I continue sipping my vanilla iced latte with skim milk in the back seat of the car. My order is the same as Mom's. I look forward and watch our lives pass us by, and one day, maybe I'll be in a car just like this one, with kids of my own, and I'll be just like my mother. We drive the remaining distance, listening to Mom's favorite playlists, and we all sing along like we're best friends.

Mom's second boyfriend after Samuel is Connor.

Much larger and stupider than Samuel, he works in chemical engineering, a fact that is confusing, given Connor didn't know bleach and rubbing alcohol mixed together make chloroform. We had to call the Poison Control Center once. Connor has two children: Johnny and Betty.

Johnny, the oldest, is a college dropout who recently decided to dedicate his life to the art of selling weed behind Walmart and working on cars in between his drug dealings. Betty tried to kill herself, so I haven't seen her much recently. She's in rehab somewhere, although I do like her. She's very smart.

Mom insisted we become a blended family, so Connor and his two children moved across the state into our Mom's house a few months ago. There's not enough bedrooms, and Mom promised us privacy, so Connor's children squeeze into one large room with a makeshift divider in between. There, they spend most of their time, disassociating from my sisters and me.

Vanessa is now sixteen and tells me Johnny, who just turned twenty-one, scares her because he's always flirting with her. She told me once he tried to kiss her in the car, so she punched him in the dick. "That sick pervert will get what's his."

"Fuck him," I replied.

It's a Monday night and only we are home, and from down the hall, the screaming starts. Bridget, Vanessa, and I listen on from the living room as another fight begins to brew. "Fuck you, fuck this shit, fuck all of it." Mom starts screaming in fury, a collected rage centered toward Connor and his idiocy, no doubt.

"What the fuck—" she continues to swear, "—are these photos?"

"Ooh, this is gonna be good," Vanessa says.

Bridget sighs at Vanessa's cynicism. "Be kind."

"I am," she reassures our sister.

Tearing through walls, Mom chases Connor outside of our house, screaming in uncontrolled, unfiltered, pure anger. In her favorite black robe, Mom's hair is done up in a towel bun, also a black towel, and wears her fluffy slippers with unicorns that Connor bought as a gift once.

"It's not what it looks like—"

"Not what it looks like? You fucking pervert! Oh, you have no idea what you have just done, just wait and see—"

"Katie—"

"Don't you dare call me by my name," Mom seethes. Her teeth grind against one another, her body so rigid, her shoulders are clenched into her neck. Connor backs down like a sad dog, desperate to fetch a bone, and runs to his car. I'm scared of his car because I found a gun in it once. He turns on the ignition and zooms out of the driveway. I can breathe again. We all watch in awe.

"Mom—" Vanessa starts.

Mom barrels towards us with her arms out desperate for our love. "He cheated," she sobs out. "I cannot believe this is happening again. I told myself this would be different." Mom's lips quiver and her strength is broken down into bits across the living room carpet. We console her by the fire, dimly lit, and tell her everything is going to be okay.

"We love you, Mom," I say.

"We're here for you," Bridget says.

"We'll ruin him," Vanessa declares.

And through her sobs, Mom blows snot into the black towel that was around her head, now being used as a handkerchief. "Yes." She mutters. "Yes, we will."

Soon after, we take part in a family affair: chucking Connor's old clothes out the car window while driving down Route 45. Vanessa takes great joy in such an excursion, tossing raggedy t-shirts and worn jeans out into the abyss. With apprehension, I throw a pair of torn-up white sneakers. Bridget refuses to participate in the family affair. "Men deserve nothing," Mom says, and we cheer her on. Men do deserve *nothing*.

Only two weeks later, Connor is living in our house again as if nothing happened. He rubs Mom's shoulders in the kitchen shirtless, his pot belly and gargoyle tattoos staring me down while I try to eat my cereal. Mom rubs his shoulders back and he lifts her in the air to kiss her, spinning her around while she giggles like a teenager. Connor and Mom are best friends again.

"I'm gonna lose my appetite," Vanessa says.

"Me, too," I reply.

"As long as Mom's happy," Bridget sighs. Even she is starting to lose faith in our Mom.

———

CONNOR FILLS the spot for Mom's third, fourth, fifth, and sixth boyfriends. Each time they break up, Connor comes back as an allegedly changed man. He's going to do things differently, he insists. And each time he says this, Connor comes back as Connor.

Mom tosses his clothes out the window of the car and Connor comes back. Connor cheats on Mom; she sends his nude photos that another girl received to his father, brother, and best friend in an email chain labeled "*cheater*". Even in the wake of their engagement party, Mom burns all the engraved wooden dishes with their initials on them in the yard during the midst of a particularly bad spat. The smoke billows through the air and Mom dances around the fire like a witch brewing a potion. "These goddamn spoons with our initials on them. What a joke."

Vanessa, now a senior in high school, cheers Mom on. "Burn them." Vanessa pours olive oil into the fire because she read online that it can heighten the flames. In the darkness, we support Mom because that's why we are family. One person's burden becomes all our burdens, and we see fit to support Mom in any way we can.

She wears a black dress, symbolic of the death of her relationship with Connor. She wears dark red lipstick because Connor always hated it when she wore dark lipstick, and she wears her flats. He preferred it when she wore high heels because he's very tall.

Freedom reclaimed, the fire grows, and as a family, our catharsis grows, too. Mom is on fire again, having remembered who she was. Her eyes are witch hazel, and her body moves like the river down by the bottom of our driveway. She twirls and sings, and together, our family dressed in black, dances around the fire, screaming freely.

"You know what?" Bridget yells out in unfiltered glory.

"What?" we all chant back.

"Fuck Connor."

"Woooooo," Mom claps her hands to her youngest daughter's words, shouting out defiant "woos" into the sky.

"We are always family," she says. "And as family, we stick together."

We cheer her on, a collection of mixed emotions as we shout toward the stars. Vanessa is pure fury, hotter than flames. Bridget is free, a symbol of hope, and more kind than me. And I am neutrality. I let Mom run away with her antics because what choice do I have? Mom is like a ship, and I cannot stop her from sinking, even if I tried.

Mom looks over the fire with glee. Her eyes are so vengeful, so tired. Her body is reclaimed by the rejection of Connor, but I doubt she's clean. The fire builds and builds, but I question how long until the flames fizzle out, or if I hold out hope, the chance this is *it*. Could this be the return of my mother? Is she coal to burning wood, orange metal incapable of fading to room temperature?

"Gather around, my children," Mom ushers us closer. Skin to skin, bone to bone, my family unite as one. "You know what to do," she nods reassuringly, and we all nod back.

"On three." Mom whispers.

"On three," I reply.

"On three," my sisters say.

"One." We pause. "Two." We whisper in unison. "Three." Big breaths in and—

"Fuck Connor."

———

"Look who's moving back in," Mom claps her hands with joy. At the door, three days after our bonfire, Connor holds his new suitcase. He bought it three breakups ago so the suitcase isn't so new anymore. This is Mom's seventh boyfriend. Connor has a buzz cut now so it's as if he's a new man. She rubs his shiny head like she just won a prize at the carnival. "My special man," she calls him.

Mom and I fight in her room while Connor goes on a grocery run. "You gotta be kidding me. Why? Again?"

My mother sits by her makeup drawer, drawing on eyeliner and doing herself up with a bright red lipstick. "You'll understand when you're older. Love is very complicated."

"*This* isn't love," I shout. My feet dig into the checkered tile floors, my face burnt red with disappointment. "You have broken up with Connor over seven times. This is unfair to us at this point. You can't keep making empty promises."

"I'm not asking you to do anything," Mom spits. She continues to brush out her hair and do her makeup while I yell. Her fiery red hair taunts me, and my anger only grows. "I'm asking for you to support my decisions. Is that too much to ask for?"

"Yes," I scream, stomping my feet and losing control

of my temper. Like a lost child, years of animosity rise to the surface. All my anger is directed towards my mother. "Why would we ever, in a million years, support your decisions? Seriously, that is a laughable question. They've led us nowhere, and we are tired. All I ask is that you listen to us, that you accept what I'm trying to say, but no. You're incapable of accountability. You're incapable of listening to me, or Bridget, or Vanessa, and we are all tired. You're being a selfish bitch." Words exit my mouth before I think of what I'm saying, and there is no word more foul to Mom than *bitch*.

"Oh, Ozzy, watch yourself." Mom still refuses to look at me, only acknowledging herself in the mirror, watching the way her lips purse as she talks coldly. "Don't you dare call me, your mother, the very woman who birthed and raised you, a bitch. Do you know all that I do for you? All that I've ever done for you? Don't test my patience."

"Is that a threat?"

"I'm just saying watch your mouth," Mom barks.

Lit to flames and incapable of being out, I'm just like my mother. I'm on fire, too. "It's true, though," I say. "You're being a selfish *bitch*." My words are nuclear— explosive. "We have to deal with you and Connor again? What happened to the time we burned all his shit? What about when we threw his clothes out of the car on Route 45? What about all the times he cheated on you?"

Mom's voice is blank. "He's a changed man."

"He just got a fucking buzz cut. Connor is the same man, you are just blind to who he is. Are you kidding me,

Mom? I don't know how else my words can get into your head. Please just do this, end this, for your kids. Please."

Mom finally spins around in a pink swivel chair, makeup placed on the counter and her eyes set ablaze. "I am going to date and do whatever I please. You are the child here. I am an adult. Don't question my decisions. Have faith in me."

"What is there to have faith in with you anymore? I have none. I have no expectations or hopes for you as a mother anymore. We are losing you. We are losing our mother and our family."

"Get out, get out, get out," Mom says with a vengeance and inability to listen, screaming, practically shattering the lights with her temper. She shrieks in mania at me over and over again until Vanessa and Bridget run to the bathroom.

"What's the matter?"

Mother seethes at her nightstand, watching us through the reflection. "Get out. All of you."

We turn to leave as one entity, one group of siblings up against our selfish, unamused mother.

"C'mon, guys," I say to my siblings. "Let's go."

There is no point in trying to ask my mother to change. Sometimes people are not capable. Or worse, sometimes people can change but won't. Control leads to no destination.

————

I GRADUATE high school this year. My older sister, Vanessa, is going into her junior year of college, and Bridget, who is now facing the worst of high school, is about to be a junior, too. Mom's been reading a lot more these days. Her final breakup with Connor was messy, and she decided to get back to her roots. She recently bought a new book about healthy relationships. She also adopted a cat. His name is Rocker and he's orange. Mom has a special gray blanket he loves. He's always kneading biscuits and making bread with his paws.

It's her newest child—her fourth. Rocker's main purpose, as Mom continuously says, is to fill the void left by my leaving. But I'm not so sad about leaving anymore. As a child, I used to lie awake staring into the universe, terrified for these days. But now, all I can think about *is* leaving.

Adulthood calls to me. Authority and independence are my source of absolution. Perhaps that's because I never got to truly live a childhood, or maybe it's because it was such a theatrical display that I'm in desperate need of change. I'm ready to be an adult.

I am not so angry at my mother anymore. We used to fight a lot about Connor and all of her boyfriends, really, but I have no fight left in me. She is single again, learning to re-love herself, and has been much kinder over the past couple of years. She's starting to remind me of the mother I knew when I was little, the one who used to read to me and tell me she loved me more than all the stars in the universe. I've accepted her for who she is and nothing more: a loving woman cursed with a desire to love cruel men.

Lying in bed, I drift off. I graduate high school in a week, and soon, I'll be moving far away to California like

Vanessa. We'll be down the street from each other and I can start fresh. Soon enough, according to plan, Bridget will join us there, too, where all of us will be together. Where we will be a family once again.

Two knocks on my door cut through the silence. "Can I come in?"

It's Mom. I clear my throat. "Yeah, of course."

Mom saunters into my childhood bedroom, floating her way over to lie beside me in bed. My star machine, my little mechanical robot projecting space throughout my room, still murmurs in the corner. The stars are dimmer now, older, but they still shine atop my ceiling, still there to catch me when I'm wandering through space.

Her curly hair is loose, no longer constantly being straightened for her lover's approval, and Mom adorns a new robe—a white one she bought after the final breakup with Connor. She wanted to switch up her routine and also her color palette.

She climbs beside me into bed, heaving out, lying flat. "Do you remember the days we used to lie awake staring at these very stars?" She leans into my shoulder. Collarbone and soft skin serve their purpose.

"How could I forget?" I smile. "Those were the best days of my life."

"Surely, not the best days," she whispers. "They were good days."

"No, those were the best days. At least the best days so far."

Mom looks up at me now, inquisitive. "Is that so?"

Sighing out, I nod, still staring into space. "I'd say so."

"Oh," Mom closes her eyes and breathes. Heavy and deep, Mom lets the air sink out of her chest and breathes in lightly.

"I suppose I made some mistakes when raising you and your sisters." She leans in closer now, and I can smell her breath, mint gum, and blue Listerine. "And I suppose," she sighs out again. "That I could've been a better mother."

I remain silent.

"But all of that aside, there is no one in this world I love more than you. My word will always remain true. You guys are my whole universe, and I love you more than this entire ceiling, world, universe, all combined. You have no idea how much I love you."

"I know how much you love me, and I love you, too." I carefully choose my words. "But our childhood, I don't think, was very easy. And I think I grew up a little faster because of it."

"I know—"

"I wish I could've enjoyed my childhood more," I interrupt. "I wish I didn't grow up so fast."

She whispers a soft 'I'm sorry', but I continue to speak. "But none of that matters anymore, I don't think. I don't feel it anymore. It's just indifference now. All of it. It's all—" I gasp for air. "Indifferent."

Mom starts to tear up again.

I once thought my Mother was a non-emotive person, someone incapable of understanding. But now I think she's quite easy to understand. Emotions rule her, and I'm scared they rule me, too. I choose indifference to soften my edges.

Mom's head rests on my shoulder, tense with anxiety, and I look away as she cries lightly in the dark. "I'm sorry," she mumbles. "I'm so sorry."

"Don't apologize. It's all okay now. I understand."

She sniffles. "I wish I could do better."

"We still have our whole lives." I lean closer to my mother as if it's all I'll ever know. "I forgive you."

Holding her like Venus, wishing she could still cradle me while I drift between Earth and Mars, we lie in the quiet while she soothes me to sleep. "I love you, baby," she says. "I love you, I love you, I love you." Both our shoulders loosen. "And I'm so sorry."

"Don't apologize," I reassure her. "You tried your best. You tried, and you were good." I don't know if my Mom was always a good mother, but I know deep down that she *is* good.

"Good." Mom mumbles the word, staring off into space. "All I ever wanted to be was good." Her words are even softer now, as if she isn't even speaking to me, but herself.

I tighten my grip around Mom, embracing her as we prepare to explore the stars.

I cannot help but hold on tight to her love as she soothes me to sleep like I'm a child again. Despite the pain she has caused us, despite the chaos of her boyfriends, I do not blame her. This is my mother, and I cannot help but cherish her love like it's ambrosia.

I'm in space again. It's so beautiful here. So quiet— endless. The green dots dance and move across the universe, and I fly through distant times and endless hours. My mom's asleep, too, nestled into my bed. I hold onto her and see her more clearly now. We are supposed to know how to figure out the world, but all we know is this: everything is a first. My mom is learning how to live for the first time, too. I am just a child learning. I crave adulthood but want the safety of my childhood forever.

Instead, I'm drifting past the Milky Way. Earth and Mars disappear into the distance, simply dots in the dark. Bright lights up ahead. It's Jupiter and Saturn. I dance along Saturn's ring as I continue towards Neptune, where I'll ascend farther and farther. For infinity, I float through the universe, bouncing from one green dot to another until I find my mom amid the stars. I'm safe here —untouchable.

"Ozzy," she shouts out, waving to me. Mom wears a white dress and drifts towards me with her arms out.

"Mommy," I shout back in relief.

We embrace for a hug, as if no time passed at all. I'm still a child. I'm still the same boy I was all those years before, chubby and naive, learning to read for the first time in the same bed. My mother, despite the years of changing her hair, clothes, and personality to fit the style of the men she loved, despite her chaos, is always going to be my Mommy.

Together, we drift deeper off to sleep and explore space, learning what it means to be alive for the first time.

6

FIRST DAY OF SCHOOL

"Smile for the camera," Mom says.

Every year, Mom insists on taking a photo of you in the driveway, right in front of the tree the neighbors want chopped down, and where you've stood in the same place year after year for the school bus. Behind schedule, you sit in the back of the bus and watch the streets pass and the lights blink green, yellow, and red, until you reach an ugly brick building with dated murals and dead bushes.

Your story, as you have come to learn, is no different from anyone else's. Your dreams are common—others crack jokes at your ambition—and you smile extra wide so your teacher will like you. Your shoes are new, your shirt is clean, and Mom helped you pick out your shorts because you weren't sure what color goes best with blue. The answer is beige. So you walk to class with your best friend, Hailey. She has fiery, sunlit hair and hazel eyes, and boys smile at her in the hallway and tap her on the shoulder when the teacher isn't looking. When they turn their heads toward you, they roll their eyes and mouth unfamiliar words.

You don't mind when the boys give you weird looks, though. You're used to it. You understand you're different, and you're still not quite sure how, but the other boys do not like you, and probably never will. So you work really, really hard and win over your teacher's approval, and tell yourself the solution to all your problems is indescribable success. If the other boys will never like you, then at least you can become really, really good at something and it won't matter so much.

Years pass, and the cycle continues as times change. A school bus turns to a car, and a playground turns towards navigating a desolate hallway for a place to eat lunch. Friendships, like the ones you had with Hailey, are gone. She chose the boys who called you mean names years before. You now know what they were calling you, and sometimes you wish you remained ignorant. Even worse, you now understand why they called you those words, and you now know they were right.

So you sit in your home on the weekends and cozy up to piles of pillows and two dogs who love you so, and wish for the life you watch on television screens.

Boy falls in love with Girl. High school romance. Diners and parties and late-night swims in a pool that belongs to your friend with the wealthy parents. Prom dates, large friend groups, and wild, reckless freedom. You wish for all you do not have, desperate to be part of a world that looks at you like an outsider. You swallow your pride and wish for the day everything changes.

You're now in college, and while everything has

changed, you still struggle to see if anything's really different at all.

You walk to class, and while you now have friends and a life and people who care about you, you're still nervous, just like you were all those years before. Excitement beats in your chest. Apprehension fills your gut. You are most nervous for the singular moment you enter the classroom. Will you be judged? Will you meet new friends? Will the class go well? The questions are endless, but you swallow your fears and plaster on a smile as you walk through the doors.

The class is full of young faces and kind eyes, and you relax in your seat as the minutes pass. A beautiful, copper haired boy sits next to you, his hair color is the same as a girl you once knew in middle school. You blank on a name—it started with an H?

He says *hi* to you, and you say *hi* back. He watches you when you stare ahead, and you look at him when he looks ahead. A part of you wonders if this is how boys and girls and girls and boys meet. Is it as simple as an exchange of conversion, and then either Boy or Girl asks for the other's number, and that's how relationships are born? You're not entirely sure because you've never experienced it yourself. It's not because you're unattractive.

For the first time in your life, you actually feel beautiful. It's because you're not like them. Boys who like boys are not hit on in public, you've learned. It's not because you do not want to, you do, but it's because you're scared. What if something goes wrong? What if they take it the wrong way? Did you imply something negative by assuming that a boy could possibly like another boy? The questions are scary, and you choose a life of solace rather than a life of fear.

But maybe this boy is different. You talk for a while, and as you build up the courage to ask for his number—maybe we can study together, is your method of choice—when another person steps in. A beautiful girl, who probably has zero intention of becoming an object of your resentment, starts to chat with the boy. He smiles at her and immediately asks for her Snapchat.

"We should study together," he tells her.

"We should definitely study together," she winks back.

And while you smile and watch two other lives connect, you're purely filled with defeat. It's not that you're mad at the boy. It's not the boy's fault, nor is it the girl's—it's simply your own. If you were like them, your life wouldn't be what it is now. The pain may have shaped you, but you fear you've missed out on a childhood. You fear you've missed out on living.

I am now twenty years old and proud of the person I've become. But even so, I am angry for my childhood. I never got to live when all I was told to do was live, and I'll never get the time back. I'll never be quite as young, and the life I want is not entirely possible. I've made peace with who I love, but I also accept the truth that the relationship between Boy and Girl is far simpler than any relationship between Boy and Boy. In the meantime, I'll make the most of these last first days as if it's all I have left.

7

GOODBYE TO BOYHOOD

IN A DINER on the corner of St. Regis Road and Valley Way, Alexander Clemens and his best friend Patrick Fairsworth sit and drink milkshakes over cheeseburgers. Every Friday after school, the two boys find themselves here: the old-fashioned diner with puppets from the 'fifties lining the walls. The floors are blue and white checkered tile, and a broken jukebox lingers in the corner. They've become well acquainted with the diner. There's even a Polaroid of the two boys on the wall alongside all the other pictures of friends, couples, and lovers from years before.

It's a combination bred from early childhood. Alexander met Patrick during baseball practice in the fourth grade. Patrick, a sports fanatic at that, was destined to be the best player out of everyone in the Little League. Alexander, on the other hand, was only playing baseball to impress his parents. It was either basketball or baseball, and he chose to be outside for the summer so he could at least get a tan.

Their friendship was a coincidence. In a heated game in July, indifferent Alexander was running to third base when Patrick, wide-eyed and determined to win, tried to tap him out. The boy in red fell to the ground face-first and Patrick stopped playing mid-game to check on Alexander. Their friendship soon bloomed, furthered by the fact that the boys had the same homeroom the following year in the fifth grade. Years passed and seasons changed, and the boys grew closer.

They belonged to different social spheres but broke the barrier as friends. Some of Patrick's friends claimed Alexander was different, *gay* even, but Patrick never cared. "He's my friend," was always his reply. "From years ago and now and always, Alexander is my best friend."

Even Alexander's friends were wary of such a friendship. "Patrick is a popular douchebag. Why are you two friends?"

Alexander's answer was simple. "Because Patrick is my best friend. From years ago and now and always." The boys had matching answers and laughed at the fact that their whole world, besides them, questioned their relationship. Patrick and Alexander never seemed to care about popularity, but such indifference made Patrick a star. He rose through the rankings of middle school and by the time high school started, Patrick was the star varsity player as a freshman.

Alexander went in a different direction. He was a writer, and unlike Patrick, excelled in school. The boys still found time for each other, though, collecting moments in the silence of a diner that had long been forgotten. The cheeseburgers were cheap, and their weekly Friday nights routine.

Tonight is no different.

The two boys sit across from each other in a red booth, Alexander slurping away on an Oreo shake while Patrick steals sips from him, opting for the diner's classic vanilla. Their conversations flow like water and they love one another like brothers, more even. "So," Alexander says through thick slurps. "What's happening with Rebecca Peters?"

Rebecca Peters is a girl in Patrick's science class, and he openly admits to having a crush on her. Alexander supports Patrick in his endeavors of infatuation but a very small part of him, microscopic even, is jealous. If Patrick starts dating Rebecca Peters, what becomes of their special Friday nights? Alexander would no longer be Patrick's best friend, and he dreads such a dilemma.

"Oh, you know," Patrick leans forward and takes a sip out of Alexander's straw.

"Not you mooching off my milkshake."

"They did a better job with yours than mine today," Patrick says, hands still pressed to Alexander's shake.

"Fuck off, drink your own milkshake," Alexander says, shoving away at Patrick from across the table.

"No. You fuck off." Patrick shoves Alexander back.

In these moments, the boys always lock eyes. It's an unspoken language, one neither of them is quite able to understand. With blurred vision and glossed over eyes, Patrick crouches into himself. The confident, talkative Patrick Fairsworth goes shy. It's a feeling of assured safety. He can't explain it, but Alexander makes him feel safe.

Alexander notices Patrick's hair in these moments. Dark brown and curly, temptation is feral, and Alexander wants to rub his fingers through it. Cheeks sharper than glass, Patrick has four dimples and a narrow-framed nose. He's always a little pink around the eyes, and freckles dance around his face.

He wishes in these glimpses to kiss Patrick, too. Alexander is aware that it's not a normal fantasy for best friends to wish for such a dream, but Patrick washes away his fear. Alexander needs to kiss him, and he thinks, as resistant as Patrick is, he wants it, too.

"So." Patrick cuts through silence. "I think I'm going to ask Rebecca out on a date."

The warmth in Alexander's cheeks goes flush, and he forces his jaw back into place. Alexander has an underbite and always finds himself correcting it, only loosening the muscles in his face around Patrick. "Oh." He claps his hands together, wiping his adoration with a smug smile. "That's great!"

"Yeah." Patrick yawns, looking away towards the broken jukebox. He reads guilty, his shoulders hunching over and his smile more awkward than ringing true. "I think I'll take her here, actually."

"Oh!" Alexander fakes another laugh. "To our diner?"

"I mean…" Patrick plays with a straw wrapper in between his fingers, rolling the paper up and then straightening it out—over and over again. "…it's not *our* diner. We just happen to go here."

"A lot."

Patrick continues to play with the straw wrapper,

incapable of staring at Alexander. "Yeah." He sighs. "I suppose. What do you think, though?"

His voice lingers in the empty diner and Alexander wishes to be honest. He wishes to tell his best friend he wants to kiss him and he should forget about Rebecca altogether. "I think it's great," Alexander says, reluctantly. "Do what makes you happy."

Patrick heaves out in relief, the color returning to his cheeks. "Ahh, thanks, man. I appreciate you."

"Anytime," Alexander forces a smile through gritted teeth. "You're my best friend. I always want you to be happy."

"Likewise. I always want you to be happy. *Man*." Patrick throws the word "man" in at the end of his words, an awkward habit that only occurs when he's uncomfortable. One time, Alexander counted Patrick using the word "man" over forty times in ten minutes at their eighth-grade snowball dance while talking to a group of girls. He was *that* nervous.

"Always, *man*," Alexander says.

"Fuck me, I'm saying 'man' too much again." Patrick slaps his hand to his face, shrinking in embarrassment.

"Yeah, *man*." Alexander puffs up his voice deeply like he's some gym bro taking way too much testosterone.

The two sit in the diner for the remainder of the night, pushing past their awkwardness and returning to being best friends. Patrick loves Alexander's long, boyish hair that reaches past his eyes in constant need of a haircut. His face is round and soft, his nose button-like, with small ears. Patrick also likes that he's taller than Alexander by almost a foot. Barely 5'9, Alexander is several inches shorter than Patrick's nearly-6'4 stature. The dynamic always results in Alexander looking up at Patrick, even when they're sitting.

As the night comes to a close, Patrick, as if practically whispering, gives a nod to Alexander. It's an understanding that even in the quietest of moments, they are always going to be best friends. It's always going to be *Patrick and Alexander.*

"From years ago and now and always, you're my best friend," Patrick says, cheeks rosy with devotion.

Alexander reiterates his words. "From years ago and now and always, you're my best friend."

Their friendship lingers past drunken milkshakes and cheeseburgers swallowed whole, and acceptance washes over the boys. The two boys, like puzzle pieces, match with one another and always will. Through passing nights, sitting at the window booth in the little diner on the intersection of St. Regis Road and Valley Way, the love the two boys have for one another only grows.

Three Months Later

IN A DINER on the corner of St. Regis Road and Valley Way, Patrick Fairsworth and his girlfriend Rebecca Peters sit and drink milkshakes over cheeseburgers. Every Friday after school, the boy and girl find themselves here in the old-fashioned diner with puppets from the 'fifties lining the walls. The floors are blue and white checkered tile, and a broken jukebox lingers in the corner. They've become well-acquainted with the restaurant. There's even a Polaroid of the couple on the wall alongside all the other pictures of friends, couples, and lovers from years before, including an old photo of Patrick with his distant best friend, Alexander Clemens.

The duo of best friends haven't spoken as much since Patrick had gotten the girl of his dreams, Rebecca Peters. She's the subject of everyone's fascination. Behind her silky, long, blonde hair and green eyes is the brain of genius.

Rebecca is at the top of their class, excelling in science, literature, and math beyond comprehension. She even takes classes at the local college down the street, Western Regional University. She's allegedly also kind. Altruistic and fair, Rebecca volunteers at the hospice for the majority of her weekends, tending to patients' bedsides and reading stories to children. She's perfect, and given such perfection, Patrick, now a junior in high school, has chosen to be a man.

When they started dating, Rebecca told Patrick he needed to start thinking about his future, which meant prioritizing what mattered most. "I do prioritize what matters most," Patrick retorted.

"Hanging out with your best friend is a distraction," Rebecca replied.

"You mean Alexander?"

"Yeah, your little nerd freak of a friend. He's a distraction, especially from any career you have. Besides, what do you two even have in common?"

Patrick went silent and only nodded his head to Rebecca's words. "You're right. I'll re-prioritize what matters most."

"Very good." Rebecca gave Patrick a thick kiss on the cheek that left a red mark of lipstick residue. As she skipped away to her next honors class, Patrick stopped texting and communicating with Alexander.

Alexander knew that it was Rebecca who had gotten in the way of their friendship. He saw it coming months before. This is what happens when anyone enters their first relationship: the world belongs to their lover, not themselves. Alexander just wished he still had a friend to call when he needed one most.

The nights they used to spend together every Friday are now spent with Alexander's dogs, Ruby and Annie—two pugs with fat faces and diabetes. They need to take shots every day. The dogs fill the void left by Patrick, and he watches movies with them in each arm throughout the weekend. He used to love watching movies with Patrick, but now Patrick is gone, so all he has is himself. Friendship is a myth. Love is a lie. Alexander is entirely alone.

Even in school, Patrick pretends to not know Alexander. They never talk in the hallways, and when they brush by one another, Alexander is a distant stranger. They always lock eyes, and Patrick's body shrinks into itself at the sight of his old best friend. His lips curl and his eyebrows furrow. He practically trips over his feet. Alexander is Patrick's liability, a constant reflection of his guilt and poor choices, and both the boys know it. Alexander wonders if Patrick wants to say he's sorry, but he doesn't. And maybe he never will.

Two More Months Gone

SUMMER IS NEAR. It's the month of May, and Alexander has spent the majority of his junior year of high school alone. Patrick, meanwhile, has been lost in his love, completely indifferent to his long-time best friend. It's another Friday night, and Ruby and Annie are having zoomies through Alexander's room.

Paws to wood, the dogs run in circles, scrambling before their next diabetes shots. Alexander scrolls through the potential options of movies to watch. He's been on a real Golden Age kick, deciding a month ago he is going to watch all of the classics. The last movie he watched was *Singin' in the Rain* and tonight he plans on watching *Casablanca*. Alone.

His phone buzzes. It's a special buzz, a special ringtone reserved for Patrick. With a loud clashing of symbols and monkeys screaming, he and Patrick gave each other matching ringtones in a fit of laughter during their freshman year after getting high for the first time and declaring custom ringtones to be the funniest thing ever created. The monkeys screech and the symbols clap, and he knows it's Patrick. The text is simple: *We need to talk. Can I come over?*

Reluctantly, Alexander wants to say no. Patrick cannot crawl his way back into Alexander's life after disappearing for five months. Who does he think he is? Another voice creeps into his mind. It's not just any person. It's Patrick Fairsworth.

Fine. You can come over. His thumb hesitates before

pressing send, but upon closing his eyes, Alexander sends the text.

I'll be over in 15.

In the dew-covered evening, spring is coming to a close. The bloated earth brings new flowers, and a sorrow-eyed Patrick Fairsworth stands on the stoop of Alexander Clemen's house. Patrick used to always rush through the door without knocking. He would climb the stairs manically up towards Alexander's room on the left, and would burst through the door, jumping on the bed to catch up with his best friend.

Instead, Patrick kicks at his shoes, a pair of black Converse Rebecca bought him for his birthday, and knocks apprehensively. His knuckles are sweaty, and despite being so tall, Patrick has never looked so short. Alexander waltzes slowly to open the door, weary of the boy who was once his best friend.

Door wide open, the two boys stand in silence. Alexander goes stoic, incapable of feeling anything when looking at Patrick. He's numb, exhausted even, and unsure of what Patrick wants. His love for his best friend has been tested, and he's not sure he can let him back in again. "Hey," Patrick finally says, throwing his hand in the air to wave.

Alexander flinches when he moves forward. "Oh, um, hey," he mumbles.

"Can I come in?" Patrick asks.

Alexander hesitates before gesturing for him to enter. "I suppose."

Brushing shoulders as Patrick walks through the

door, Alexander struggles to even look him in his eyes, opting to stare at the hardwood caramel floors instead.

"So." Patrick bites at his lip and plays with his hands. "It's been a while, *man*."

"Yeah," Alexander says through a clenched jaw. "Go figure."

"So we're just jumping right into it then, huh," Patrick says.

Alexander snickers, but it's an angry laugh at that. There is nothing funny here. "Hmm, I don't know, Patrick. What happens when one day your best friend ghosts you? No warning, no texts, no calls. They just go rogue. And then you try to make an effort at reaching out to them, but no! They do not reply. And I know it's because of your girlfriend so I was happy to give you the space to figure out whatever the fuck that was, but no.

"I haven't heard from you in over five months. And at school, you don't even look at me or talk to me, and you treat me like I'm something lesser than you. Like I'm not worthy of respect at all. So yeah, Patrick, we are going to go there, because I am angry. Not only am I angry but I am so fucking tired, and I want to know exactly why you came here because I really don't want to see you right now." Taking a huge gasp for air, Alexander sighs, turning away from the entrance of his home and marches towards his room in pure, unfiltered, manic rage.

Patrick stands in horror.

"Are you coming or what?" Alexander finally asks.

Without words, Patrick follows, dragging behind Alexander as he stomps his way forward. "Alexander, listen," Patrick begins.

Alexander throws himself on his bed, staring towards the television, wrapping Annie and Ruby in his arms. His little pugs bark at Patrick's arrival, familiar with the boy who used to hang with Alexander at his house weekly. In short, angry breaths, Alexander yawns at Patrick's rebuttal. "I'm listening."

"I came here to say I'm sorry. For all of it. I really fucked shit up and it's all my fault and I have nothing to say except I'm sorry." Alexander clings to the corner of the bed, wrapping his fingers tightly around camel sheets. Patrick lingers in the corner of his bedroom.

"Is that it?"

"What? No." Patrick exclaims in exhaustion. "I'm sorry for ghosting you. For listening to Rebecca when she said I need to focus on my future and less on my friends. I should've never listened to her. You are my future. I don't want a future unless you are somehow in it, like we've always planned. I'm sorry for pretending I never knew you in school. That was a real dick move. I'm sorry for just never giving you a reason why I left. There is no valid reason. I just did and I'm sorry. And I've been sorry about this for months. I just don't know how to make things right, so I thought I'd start here.

"I miss being friends with you. I miss hanging out with you. I miss going to the diner with you and only you. Not Rebecca or anyone else—you. I miss it when things were just us. And now it's all fucked."

With a great inhale, Alexander is ready for the attack. "I appreciate the sentiments, I really do, but if I'm not mistaken, you are the reason it's all fucked up."

"Well—"

"Aren't you the one who ghosted me? Aren't you the one who took everything we had in this friendship that started when we were ten years old and threw it away? And for what? A girlfriend who will drop you as soon as she gets into Harvard. You aren't her endgame. You're just a distraction. And aren't you still dating her? Does she know you're here? I'm not gonna be friends with someone who can't even be open about who his friends are to his girlfriend. Be honest. Answer the question."

Stammering over his words, Patrick locks eyes with Alexander. Cocoa to copper, the two pairs of chestnut eyes stare at each other. Alexander's shoulders relax, and his stomach drops. Sweat drips down Patrick's back and guilt eats away at his bones. The two boys are tired of fighting.

"You're right." Patrick finally exhales. "She doesn't know I'm here."

"You see—"

"Let me finish. It doesn't matter, though, because I'm gonna break up with her. If she cannot accept my friends then she cannot accept me. You, so I've come to realize, are more important to me than her. You are my brother, more even, and I don't want to lose you."

The room grows quiet. Alexander, sitting in contemplation, wishes to hug Patrick but holds himself back. He wishes they can be best friends again, sitting in the diner like it's yesterday, and all their problems can be gone. He wishes for everything to be normal again. He wishes and wishes and wishes. Dropping his hands, Alexander sits in defeat at the edge of his bed, staring up towards Patrick. "Okay."

"Okay?" Patrick repeats.

"I miss you and I miss our friendship. I miss when you were my best friend, and if what you're saying is true, I'm willing to let you back in again."

Jumping onto the bed, Patrick throws himself in Alexander's arms, reaching wide across to hug his best friend. "I'm so sorry," he wails. "I'm so, so, so sorry. I'm sorry."

Through chuckles of relief, Alexander hugs him back, his hands wrapping around Patrick's back and digging into him tightly. "I've missed you, too. It's okay. I swear. I mean it's not okay, what you did, obviously, but it's going to be okay."

The two boys hug for an eternity, and as soon as Patrick leans away, the boys realize Patrick is on top of Alexander, arms around his back. On instinct, as if it's second nature, as if it's all they know, Patrick leans in to kiss Alexander, leaning forward and letting his body drop on top of Alexander's.

Apprehensive, Alexander kisses him back, swallowing him whole and accepting his best friend has always been more to him than a brother. "Wait," Alexander pulls away.

"What is it?"

"We can't be doing this." Alexander says, although his chin now rests on Patrick's collarbone. "What about Rebecca?"

"We're over. Don't worry about it," Patrick is dismissive. He accepts these words as fact, but also out of his own lust. Alexander cannot help himself.

Patrick leans into kiss Alexander once again, two

bodies acting on feral instincts that neither one can control. Alexander is kissing alongside Patrick's neck, working his way down his chest. Patrick's breath goes short, and barely pulls away to breathe as he kisses his best friend for the first time.

In between these moments, they talk to one another tenderly. "From years ago and now and always, you'll always be my best friend," Patrick says, smiling as he buries his face into Alexander's chest.

"From years ago and now and always, you'll always be my best friend, too," Alexander replies. Legs intertwined and feet resting atop one another, the boys sleep until the morning arrives.

"Promise me you'll stick to your promises," Alexander says. It's the following morning and Patrick dresses in his clothes from the night before—a black hoodie with a white t-shirt, and those same black converse that Rebecca Peters bought him. "I promise," Patrick says, kissing Alexander goodbye on the forehead.

The following Monday, Alexander arrives at school with a smile once again. He imagines the day will go perfect. He'll walk over to Patrick's locker where they will chat about nonsense until first period. Then class. Following class, he'll find Patrick for their second class together. Afterwards, they'll hang out in study hall together, where they'll share the same music on a playlist they've been building over the last several years. It's titled *in the works,* and features all of their combined favorite music: Cage the Elephant, Paramore, Lorde's *Pure Heroine,* and M83.

But instead, perched right up against Patrick's locker

is Rebecca Peters. Her white crop top is easy to spot a mile away from down the hallway, and before he even reaches Patrick's locker, he knows such fantasies are too good to be true. Patrick is not going to break up with Rebecca Peters for him. Regardless, Alexander continues to stand his ground and walks closer to Patrick's locker.

"Hey," he says, standing before an uncomfortable Patrick with pasty white skin and a confused Rebecca, whose angry eyes and demeanor exude an energy of *I'm better than you*. She's chewing bubblegum, spearmint flavored, and it reeks from across the hall.

"Yeah?" Rebecca says, her mouth swaying left and right as she continues to chomp down on her gum.

Alexander ignores her and turns towards Patrick. This is the real test of his word. "What's up with you?"

With his eyes directed at his locker, Patrick's entire body language shifts away from Alexander as if he's some pest he needs to avoid.

"Yeah?" he says, following suit with Rebecca.

"I'm just checking in. Seeing what's up."

"Oh," Patrick says. "I'm pretty busy, *man*. Maybe we can talk later."

"Or how about never?" Rebecca chimes in, wrapping her arm around Patrick, claiming her territory.

"Right," Alexander says, swallowing his pride and wiping the hope off his face. His smile is gone, and he gives the couple a big thumbs up before he turns and darts away. The hallways extend for miles.

Pushing through seas of teenagers, Alexander runs to crouch in the corner of a bathroom stall and holds back tears. Surrounded by hand-drawn penises with sharpies and swastikas, the school bathroom is a treacherous place, and Alexander weeps into toilet paper thinner than tissue. The fantasy is shattered. The best friend Alexander once knew is gone. Patrick will never be his true best friend or anything more for that matter, ever again. All Alexander has is himself, and that has to count for something.

It's time he let go of the illusion and accept the truth. Alexander pulls himself together, wipes away his tears, and re-emerges into the hallway good as new. He is not going to let Patrick take away his happiness again.

He isn't worth it.

One Month Later

IN A DINER on the corner of St. Regis Road and Valley Way, Alexander Clemens sits alone on a summer evening, drinking an Oreo milkshake served with a cheeseburger. The boy has made a lot of memories at the diner. The floors are blue and white-checkered tile, and a broken jukebox lingers in the corner. There's even an old Polaroid of Alexander with his former friend, Patrick Fairsworth on the wall, alongside all the other pictures of friends, couples, and lovers from years before.

"Hey, boss." The server, a sixty year-old man by the name of Hugo, approaches. With a big belly stretched out, Hugo has owned his family's diner for decades and still preserves it to this day. "How you doin'?" he asks.

Alexander, in between bites of his cheeseburger, casts

a smile towards Hugo. "I can't complain. I mean, I am eating the best burger around."

"You're the best, Kid," he replies. "You've been here a lot alone recently. I was gonna ask where's that friend of yours? You know, the one with the height and super-curly hair? What was his name?" Hugo rubs his chin. "Ahh. Patrick. Patty, my boy. Where's he at?"

"Oh." Alexander twists in the booth, fumbling over the question. "Haven't seen much of him these days myself, actually."

"Is that so?" Hugo's mouth widens in disbelief. "You guys used to hang out here constantly. What happened? Did you guys fight over a girl or something?"

"You could say that," Alexander replies. "It's complicated, but I'm sure he's doing good, wherever he is. If I ever see him I'll make sure to pass along the word."

Hugo grunts. "You better. At least in the meantime, take a new photo for the wall." The man points towards the other side of the diner where all the Polaroids lie. "We gotta update it every year with some new photos. You know where the camera is."

"Thanks, Hugo," Alexander says.

Grabbing the camera from the front of the diner, tucked underneath a wooden table, Alexander centers the camera and tries to press down all the buttons at once to get a good shot. Usually, he'd have Patrick here to take the photo for him, and he'd smile nice and wide for his best friend as they took turns getting the perfect picture. But it's just Alexander, and he's okay with that.

One, two, three. *Click!* The polaroid beeps and a little piece of film slowly and surely ejects from the camera. Flicking his wrist, Alexander observes the photo form under the diner lights, watching as his smile comes into frame first, followed by his eyes. Then his cheeks, and finally, his long, brown hair.

Bright-eyed and full of hope again, Alexander is starting to feel like himself. He's now accepted the fact that he's gay, and he's probably always known it to be true, but distracted himself by mistaking lust for friendship.

His friendship with Patrick ruled his world for the majority of his boyhood, but now he's almost eighteen. He's soon going to be a senior in high school and will head off to college. Alexander, while alone, would rather stand in his own solitude than by a friend who does not uphold his word. He now knows one day someone greater will come along, and it will not be Patrick.

He knows it's time to let go.

Placing the new picture on the wall, he admires all the old photos he's taken there. There's a photo of him and Patrick after getting drunk for the first time and running through the streets in the middle of the night to down milkshakes. There are pictures of them after movies, after baseball games, after recitals where Patrick came to cheer Alexander on as he recited stories he wrote to small venues. Their entire lives are dictated by the wall, and now, the only new photos that remain are a picture of a snarky-faced Rebecca kissing Patrick on the cheek and a singular selfie of Alexander, sitting in the diner on a Friday night, eating his favorite cheeseburger and drinking an Oreo milkshake.

Alexander places the photo proudly on the wall,

examining his photography. He observes his smile. He has a thick button nose he finds beautiful. He has little ears that are tucked away by a mop of wavy brown hair atop his head. He admires his solitude, his ability to accept his loneliness as not something that makes him weak, but indicative of his strength. This is who he is, and he finally likes what he sees. He finally likes who he has become.

Sitting back down, he lets go of the past. All of it.

A new feeling rises within his belly, and it's not the remnants of cheeseburger and Oreo milkshake, which is already a deadly combo.

It's acceptance for what once was and what now is.

Alexander Clemens is going to be okay.

8

BOY

"Sex is purely transactional," Boy says.

It's three in the morning and I'm invited over to a boy's dorm. It's the beginning of February and the second semester has only begun. I told myself this semester would be different. Maybe I'll be more willing to let go of my preconceptions and allow myself to have more fun. Maybe college *is* hookup after hookup, trial and error, until you find the match that sticks—miraculously.

You think of the process that led you to Boy's room. It started with a Snapchat at three in the morning. You have a message from a familiar face. It's from Boy. Acquaintances at best, friends, if you're so willing to call him one; he texts you *hey*.

You reply *hey*.

He asks if you want to come over. If you question why, he'll press you on coming.

Come on, he'll say.

But it's late.

It's not that late. You can sleep in tomorrow.
Okay.
So that means you're coming?

You think about it. You want to ask someone else for advice but it's late, and they, too, are either sleeping or also with someone. The decision is left up to you. In pondering the question, you ask what he wants to do.

The responses will vary. *What do you think?* An angsty boy full of hormones looking for a quick release might reply. Adversely, *anything you want.* You think of how to reply. By definition, an invite to an acquaintance's room at devil's hour is a hookup. A hookup which starts as it ends, temporary and nothing more. On the other hand, you know you're desperate. You're craving love and they're craving sex. Can the two balance out? You finally oblige. You will go over to Boy's apartment at three in the morning.

How long are you gonna be?
About 10 mins.
Ok sick. 75 East Avenue, Apartment 04.

Boy lists off his address like it's some place where a package needs to be dropped. Or where divorced parents meet in a parking lot to pass off their children for the week. There's an efficiency to dropping a location with a time. It's quick, easy—transactional.

You rush to the mirror and brush out your hair. You gargle mouthwash and apply some Chapstick to your lips. You want Boy to desire you. You want Boy to love you. You layer on deodorant as if going to the gym and spray a light amount of cologne so it seems that wherever you walk, you naturally smell good. You brush your teeth, take out your retainer since you're not going to bed, and try to wake yourself up.

You look back in the mirror. You smile. Every tooth needs to be white. There cannot be any pimples. You want to look beautiful for Boy. Those who are loved are attractive, you tell yourself.

Buried thick in your winter jacket as you walk to Boy's apartment, you pass by the same streets you now consider home. The roads are quiet, the buildings dimly-lit through the dark. Snow piles in the corners of streets, dark brown in color, mixed with the grime of the city. With each step, you ask yourself if you're making the right decision. Should you go to Boy's place? Is this moment, the walk to and from Boy's apartment, worth it at all?

Intuitively, you really want to know if you're making a mistake. Are your high standards and desire to be loved normal and is everyone else simply wrong? Are your friends steering you in the wrong direction? Is the world you seek even fathomable? The questions build up like the piles of snow stuffed into corners of city blocks, so instead, you take your feelings and stuff them deep down your throat.

Boy is the right choice. Your friends are right—you need to have more fun. This is college, they say. This is what people do. This is what *you* should do. So it's exactly what you do. You swallow your pride and march your way to Boy's apartment in the dead of winter, burying your regrets before you even kiss his lips.

You now stand outside Boy's door and text him to let him know you're there.

I'm here, you write. But before you send the message, you question if you should even send it at all, ready to spin back around in your sneakers, out the doors of 75 East Avenue, Apartment 4, and wish for the walk home. You will then bury yourself in your covers, grabbing at your body, thankful you didn't waste too many breaths on a boy who only cares about you at three in the morning.

But now you wait, and you send the text.

Boy doesn't reply immediately.

He's in no rush to have you come over. You're a means to an end, a simple transaction, and he will treat you as such.

A few minutes pass by. Boy's door is a cold white, placed at the end of a narrow hallway smelling of cigarettes and grape-flavored vape juice. You contemplate knocking but you know not to. You must never knock. That might wake up the other boys who live there. Finally, you hear a sigh and the slight tapping of footsteps against a dirty, wooden floor.

There in the door light, Boy stands, staring at you with a look of intent in his eyes. He's still in his outfit from the night before—most likely a drunk celebration with his friends that ended with him feeling sexually promiscuous and now wanting you. It's a white button-up with unbuttoned navy dress pants, loosely hanging off his torso. His socks even have decorative little pizzas all over them, and you notice how nonchalant Boy is to you being there, as if a million other boys walk through the door weekly to serve Boy. You're just another body, just another thing waiting to be used, and you accept it.

"Oh, hey," Boy says, almost surprised you showed up. But you did.

"Hey." You nod your head.

Boy gives you a slight side hug, which you accept. A hug should mean nothing compared to what he wants to do to you.

"This is the place."

You scan the room around you. The kitchen is tangled in dirty dishes and brown rags hang over the sink's edge. The chairs are made of plastic, and old food containers are littered across the only table within the room. On the wall, there are sad posters of *Pulp Fiction* and *The Wolf of Wall Street*—a display of Leonardo Dicaprio spreading his arms out wide with stacks of cash flying around him in the air.

You go quiet, almost shocked you're even at Boy's apartment, and despite your trepidation, Boy doesn't care.

"My room's this way." Boy leads you to the left, opening his bedroom to another small rectangle, a full bed placed in the center of the room. A brick wall sits behind the bed—two little tables covered in knick-knacks and old soda cans lay beside it.

"You like it?"

"Yeah." You lie to Boy, hoping he doesn't see the fear in your eyes. You wish you weren't there. You wish you could turn back now, but you swallow your pride and smile. Boys like you smile for Boy because it makes you more desirable.

Boy leans back and flails his body on his bed, staring at you with his head resting against his pillow.

He places his arms behind his head, waiting for you to speak.

"Uhh, what's up?"

"Ahh nothing, just tired. Come sit." Boy pats the spot on his bed next to him, eager for you to inch your way closer.

You approach the bed and sit on its end, slowly moving back to lean against an array of pillows beside Boy without touching him. You're scared of his touch but yet you find yourself in his bed, waiting for his next move. You're already ashamed of yourself before Boy has even done anything to make you feel shameful.

"How was your night?"

Boy darts his eyes across the room and then back at you. "It was good. Some of my friends and I went out to the bars and just drank a ton, and now I'm here."

"Nice." You notice how Boy doesn't ask you about your night, or really anything at all. You decide to share information about yourself on your own accord, not because he asked, but because you wish to fill the silence. "My night was pretty chill," you continue. "I just hung out with some friends, too, and got some dinner, and now I'm here."

"I can see that," Boy replies.

"So what now?" you ask.

Boy smiles slightly and bites at his lips, thinking. You know exactly what he wants but you play dumb anyways.

"Tell me something about yourself," Boy says. As he speaks, Boy inches closer towards you, turning his body sideways on top of the charcoal covers. Boy looks right into your eyes, mirroring intimacy as if Boy likes you—as if Boy knows you. Boy practices the act of love as if he is capable of one day loving you. You wish he would.

"I don't do this that often," you say.

Boy's eyes widen.

You cannot tell if he's upset or intrigued by your inexperience. Maybe Boy finds it attractive that you don't go to other boys' apartments at three in the morning.

"No problem with that. I get it," Boy says.

"Really?"

"I mean, yeah. It's not that deep, so I just don't really allow myself to be emotional." Boy laughs in between his words. "It can be weird doing this. But don't worry, I got you."

"Thanks," you reply. "I am just a little more emotional than that."

"Ahh, I see."

"Yeah."

"Well, how's this for emotional?"

Boy, as if on cue, leans in to kiss you. Boy practices the act like a movie camera is filming him and he needs to get all the right angles and say all the right things. Boy's actions—his words, his lips, his movements are all part of a rehearsal. Boy's the star and remains the star. You become the object of desire for a mere minute and are told to accept Boy's intimacy because it's the best you will ever receive.

You kiss Boy back.

Boy leans on top of you and strips off his clothes in a swift motion. You awkwardly fumble at your hoodie to take it off, unsure of how to grab at your pants while Boy leans over you.

The night starts as it ends: temporary.

Boy has sex with you.

And after every kiss, every touch of his hands against your body, you wish to go home. You fantasize about your bed and covers. You dream of being home again as a little kid, wishing for true love when it seemed real. You wish for a time before you knew Boy and his body and when your preconceptions still mattered. But even so, you still hope afterward, he might hold you. You hope he will ask you to stay. You hope Boy will let you rest on his chest and he will kiss your forehead. You hope and hope and hope.

Despite your fears, you think about building a world with Boy. 'Maybe he will take me to dinner one of these days. Perhaps he will take me to the movies. We can have conversations about the books I like and the world he hopes to live in.' You hope he will tell you about his family, what makes him happy, and what keeps him up at night. You most desire for him to tell you he loves you—that you're no longer alone.

"I'm in love with you," Boy says. The word love falls off his lips like a bullet to the heart, explosive in all the best ways possible.

"I love you, too," you reply.

But Boy doesn't really confess his love for you. He never will.

Once Boy finishes, he dismisses you.

"I gotta go to bed," Boy says. "See you later."

This time, he doesn't give you a side hug. He opens his bedroom door, expecting you to navigate your way through his apartment on your own. You dodge plastic chairs and try to be quiet as you step across squeaky wood panels. Once you approach the front door, you open and close it yourself while Boy wraps himself tightly in his sheets.

You gather your things and stand alone outside 75 East Avenue, Apartment 04, and wish you could take it all back. Boy never cared. He wanted your body, and now you're nothing more than a finished transaction. A coupon. A CVS receipt that stretches down to the floor, your desires written on it only for it to be discarded. He said goodnight and didn't even walk you to the door.

You stand stoic in the face of Boy's door. You stare at the wood. The thick, white coats of paint cannot disguise the years of scars running down its wooden seams. You trace your finger down the door for a minute, trying to grasp what just happened.

Nothing feels real. Perhaps everything feels so real, you focus on the door to forget. To forget his body going inside of you. To forget his tongue gliding down your throat. The marks left by his mouth are littered across your neck, his way of taking claim to your existence. You think of all the ways you will take a sponge and scrub away at your skin when you go home. You want his touch gone, his marks to disappear. The door is riddled with deep grooves that no paint can cover, but you will never forget the encounter you had with Boy.

In the days following, you'll sigh out a breath of relief once his lip stains are gone. Your friends will ask what's on your neck and you will shyly admit to hooking up with Boy. Everyone will cheer you on and say how proud they are of you for getting out of your shell. *Look at you go!* They'll say. *You finally did it, we're proud*, they'll tell you. All around, your decision is regarded with laughter and praise as if you took a step closer towards adulthood, shedding your skin as a child. You're just like them now. You're liberated—you're free.

And you'll laugh at their jokes but won't feel free. The one thing you wish to say but never will is how much you regret Boy. You don't tell them how you wanted to cry every time Boy touched you. You don't want to say aloud how embarrassed you feel—how much shame you harbor. You don't tell them how Boy threw you away the minute he was finished with you, or even how every night when you crawl into bed, you find yourself reliving that one night over and over again, desperate for some sort of way to undo time.

You think of time a lot more now. There's the little boy you once were, and then there's you now. In a dream world where Boy never happened, you would still be the little boy who believed in love and kindness and the good in other boys. You still wish you were that little boy. But Boy taught you that naïveté doesn't last forever. Boy taught you the truths in the world. Boy showed you what it's like to be *loved* now, what it's like to be *touched* now.

So now you will cry and laugh and pretend but know the truth, and it's one that can't be undone. The reality of Boy is this: he's like every other boy. Boy wants you until he doesn't. You become unwanted the minute you ask for anything greater than a transaction. Then, Boy will discard you. Boy will move onto his next target and the next one after that.

To Boy, the world is easy. Sex is easy. Love is easy. Boy

wields love as a fantasy he can use to give him what he wants, which he knows you will do. Boy always wins, and you, while also a boy, are not Boy.

I am twenty-one years old and a junior in college, and I harbor more regrets now that I'm older. I wish I could take back time and undo the world for a minute, but I can't. I hope to be more than an object of desire, but we don't live in a world where that exists. I'm always going to remain a boy, used by Boy, and in the end, I'm the one who's hurt.

This is love, I'm told.

This is love.

9

BOYFRIENDS FOR THE NIGHT

January 3, 2023

Night.

"I don't believe in love these days," I say. We sit in the car, staring out at a beach the color of midnight. Rain weeps from the sky, trickling across the sand and ricocheting off the metal roof of your little red Toyota. Florida is a wetland. The bay sits three blocks from the house, an inlet full of sunken dreams and more beaches where nonexistent treasure is searched for. Gold, silver, and rubies become subjects of fascination but no longer can be found on these coasts.

Right now, the cold beach without a moon is ours. The car sits in an empty parking lot, and curiosity lingers in between our lips and interlocked hands. Your silver looped chain drapes from your neck and your eyes are warmer than symphonies. Our paths crossing was never meant to happen. This moment was never supposed to become real. I am simply in your hometown on vacation, a brief passing through before I head back to New York.

Our eyes lock, and the violins are off to the races. Fiddlestick to wood, the symphony plays from a little Bluetooth speaker in the center of your car.

"The actual speakers are broken," you say as you shrug, quickly changing the topic. "If there's nothing to believe in, then what's there to live for?"

My heart hangs from my sleeve when you look at me. I let your words linger, my shoulders dropping and my face softening. Tightness builds between my eyes, an anxiety that if I look at you long enough, this will all disappear. I reluctantly let you in. "Moments like this to prove me wrong."

Without acknowledgement, you pull your body into mine. With fingers clasping around the collar of my hoodie, you hold onto me as if I'll run. I only find myself running closer into your arms, wrapping my palms around your shoulders, fingers digging into your back. We kiss, and for the first time, it feels real. It feels how it should feel. Top lip to bottom, we fit into each other like we're made for this. I swallow your adoration, and despite my need for more of you, my only thought isn't you.

It's the truth.

———

2022

Within a bar composed of black-painted brick, candles illuminate a dark room with red leather booths. I sit in the back corner on a date from Hell. An angry voice, harsh and pointed, radiates in my ear. Each word he spits could cut through skin. It's a blind date, a combination designed by a distant class friend. Her name is Chloe, and this is her "dear friend, Ronny."

Ronny is a cruel-looking man. With clammy hands made of lard, Ronny's eyebrows are thinner than pencil lines. Whenever he smiles, it appears to materialize into a frown. He's yelling about finance on our first date. "He's in Investment Banking," Chloe had said. "Super rich and super young." Not that either of those things matter, but success is refreshing. Especially in men. I find myself to be a tough critic, so scared to let people in, sometimes I'm more judgmental than I need to be. But given Ronny, my criticisms are pertinent.

"That woman I work with is such a fucking bitch, you have no idea," Ronny huffs.

He's almost coked out, his eyes so wide they could squeeze out of his head and fall atop the table. I imagine such a scenario because even his eyes falling out would be more interesting than this conversation. "We both have to compete for the same clients, and she just is a whore, and that's how she gets her clients. Fucking *cunt.*" There's the knife. He speaks so sharply the very wooden table where we sit could splinter in three.

With chills down my spine, I try to stay calm and please Ronny. I try to make it through the date. "Right." I fake a laugh, forcing my teeth to clamp down together. I have an underbite and push my jaw back so my smile is more appealing to Ronny. I don't know why I do this, but I find myself always rearranging my jaw, cracking it into place for better inspection. "So how is everything else going?" I redirect the conversation.

"I have a Grindr thing after this so that should clear my head."

My cheeks sour and my hands go numb. I don't know why I'm angry. Maybe it's his lack of respect. I am next to nothing to Ronny, and if he—a man—sees me like this, then I suppose all do. I bite my tongue and fake another smile, letting him continue on another rant.

"It's like shopping a market," he says. "There's an endless array of bodies. I love it."

Burrowing deeper into my navy sweater, I cover every ounce of skin. The table beneath my arms is sticky, so I let my sweater cling to the wood as a distraction. I'll throw it in my dirty hamper later—the corner of my room— and I'll shower, soon ridding myself of Ronny. Only a few more minutes to go.

The angry man's right hand clasps at his beer like it's water and he's in the desert, desperate for rescue. Taking a large swig back, he wipes his lips with his crack-covered tongue, licking at his face while staring at me. I'm another piece of meat for him. "You're welcome to join too, you know."

The conversation goes stale, and I leave soon after. I kiss Ronny on the cheek, telling him I had an *amazing night,* and *can't wait to see him again.* He puffs his chest out in pride and stumbles away to Brooklyn where he'll have his next Grindr hookup. I head home and shower intensely, scrubbing until I bleed. The truth, so I've come to learn, is men do not care. They just want sex, never love.

I'm no exception.

January 2, 2023
Afternoon.

Sitting on the outer bay of a coastal town in Northern Florida, I arrive on January 2nd to escape the chaos of my world. The offer came to me suddenly. A friend of a friend had a house with a pet turtle that needed watching. His name is Rocky, named after the iconic movie character, Rocky Balboa. He's a green little man with half a tank dedicated to swimming and the other half a dirt patch where Rocky lounges after rough matches in the ring. All expenses paid for, I quickly sign on to watch Rocky—a very low-maintenance animal— for four days.

The home sits in desolation.

Roaming an abandoned house, I am alone. It's an aquatic home, decorated with lots of teal and framed quotes about the importance of love and family. *Family: where life begins & love never ends.* The framed signs always swaps the "and" for the more aesthetic alternative, an "&" symbol.

I'm already bored. I open dating apps to explore. Curiosity often wins and patience isn't my strong suit. The swiping goes dull and my thumb matures into lethargy. The apps only show me men who remind me of Ronny. But then, through the midst of older men and young men, all looking for sex and nothing more, there's you.

I notice your hair first. Long waves of black flow past your forehead and practically cover your eyes. You have two studs for earrings—both silver—and a small nose that I find myself practically envious of. You stand in a red sweater with crossed arms, smiling into the camera, looking past the lens. Your eyes light up so wide. You, I am so sure, are good. I swipe right.

It's a match!

You message me first a few hours later. *Hey! Do you have anything fun planned for today?*

I reply within five minutes. *Nope. Just got to Florida for four days and I've never been here before. Haha.* I throw in a "haha" towards the end of the text to soften the blow. I want you to ask me out, and to do so of your own volition. I'm too shy to ask such large questions.

Let me be your tour guide, then, you reply instantaneously.

The conversation flows hurriedly after that, evolving into you and I meeting tonight.

It's a date.

A couple hours later, you greet me for the first time in the driveway. A car of maroon, you swing by after work—you're a server at an Italian restaurant—to take me to the beach with you. The car is clean with piles of your work uniform, a black shirt and black pants, stacked in the back seat, resting against the tan interior. Your name, a yellow medallion made of plastic, shines atop the black polo shirt. In bold red letters, it reads *Arthur,* like the cartoon of the aardvark everyone mistakes to be a rabbit. You used to hate such a name. You found it embarrassing, but now you love it.

There's also a stuffed animal of Sonic sitting in the backseat, buckled in neatly like he's a third passenger.

You bought it for yourself while shopping, a present to yourself because *why not,* and now the new plush toy sits in your back seat watching our first date.

"Hey," you say as you hug me. I crawl into your little red car parked at the edge of the driveway. With a thick southern drawl, your words sound like you're talking as if you're chewing through a meal, and I like it. Your vowels are more rounded, more soft. You sound kinder than the men I know from home.

I face forward, too nervous to turn and lock eyes with you. "Hey."

I lower my voice an octave. I sink deeper into your car seat as we trek towards the water. With your left hand on the steering wheel and your right hand placed on the console in between us, I observe your fingers. You have thick wrists, probably from your years carrying food as a server, and three braided bracelets loosely tangled around your skin. It's a combination of colors—gold, silver, and red.

"You like my bracelets?" You speak so nonchalantly.

"They're pretty cool." I try to play the role of chill. Being calm has never been my strong suit. "Who made them?"

"My friend and I did a few years ago. There's a lot of treasure hunting here so we made bracelets the color of the treasure everyone talks about but no one seems to find."

You wear a black T-shirt and faded, baggy denim jeans. The silver chain shines across the edge of your neck, and I find myself looking at every part of you except your eyes. If I look too intently into your eyes, I'll grow too nervous. Observance is my resolution.

You drive fast, daring past red lights and slowing down by the places where cops lurk. Red and blue lights become my fear, but you soon park the car and hop out, rushing around to the passenger side to open my door. Extending your hand, you grab mine and pull me forward. Our chests bump into each other, and before I pull my hand away, you brush the top of my hand with your thumb.

The beach parking lot is empty, the pavement riddled with sand, and dark trees overhead cover us from the moon. It's a waning crescent, so close to not existing at all.

"Follow me," you say. Eyes of mahogany lead the way, thick lashes, and a sharp nose point in the direction towards the beach. Your body loosely strolls past the trees with a self-assured knowingness of destination.

Under a sliver of moonlight and dim parking lot lights, your back pops out of your shirt, thick muscles lie underneath. I follow in pursuit as you walk forward, nodding for me to catch up and walk alongside you. Terrified to live, I reach for you in the dark. I look for comfort in your existence as I bite away at my nails. "Are we allowed to be here?" I ask. "I'm nervous. I feel like we're sneaking or trespassing. I'm not from here. Is this alright?"

You smile. "We're not sneaking." You almost laugh at my fears, so collected, you are cooler than the winds that break from ocean waves. "We're exploring." You wave your finger in the air as if you're an astute teacher giving some lesson to a crowded room. "Those are two very different things. I got you."

You got me. We approach a wooden bench, legs buried in sand by the edge of the water. You sit to my right, and I make sure I'm towards your left. My good side is my right, so I only want you to see me from that angle.

"So," you say.

Cheeks red and fears dissipating, I nudge your side. "So."

"What's your story, *Alexander Clemens*?" You say my full name with that southern drawl, emphasizing every syllable. Your words are sincere and your question is raw.

I tap at my shoes, a pair of brown Converse, and look towards the waves as distraction. "That's a loaded question."

"We have all the time in the world."

"Well," I clear my throat, reluctantly looking towards you.

Piercing eyes stare back at me, and you watch as I fidget with the strings on my hoodie and tap at my feet.

Anxiety has always riddled my body, even now, but you don't seem to mind. Your left arm wraps around the bench and loosely drapes itself over my shoulder. Your thumb rubs my back, and you nod as you wait for me to find the courage to speak. "I'm a writer, so I want to write books."

Your face lights up with elation, a cheesy smile across your face.

You seem tempted to ask more questions, but I continue. "I find that books are the only places where my emotions feel real. It's a controlled environment, one where my aspirations come true and I can create the happy endings. It's all a product of my own design, and I like that."

"Do you find writing makes your own life easier?"

"Sometimes." I shrug at such a question. "Not easier, but makes life feel a little less chaotic. I can at least control what happens in my story since I have no control over what happens in my real life."

You lean in closer, your lips pink and your cheeks plump with adoration. "What do you write about?"

"All sorts of things," I wave my hand in the air. "College, growing up, love, relationships, fantasies. It's anything I wanna write about."

Your smile softens and your eyebrows lower. "Can I read your work?"

The question feels too personal—too real. I drop my eye contact and stare at the water again. "Maybe."

"I promise you I'll love it."

I can feel your eyes pressed to my face. Your contact does not intimidate me, but fills me with fear. Intimacy scares me. Letting people in is terrifying. Solitude provides safety but here you are like ocean waves, crashing down my walls. I reluctantly look back towards you again. "Let's talk about you now. What's your story?"

You clear your throat and laugh through the dark. Your head bobs back as you think, and your eyes lock with the stars before your gaze quickly shifts towards mine. "I play the violin, so I want to be a music teacher one day."

"Ahh, a musician," I say. "Can you play me something sometime?"

"Anything for you." Confidence carries through your voice.

We spend the rest of the night talking at the beach, staring out at the ocean with an endless horizon. The waves crash and break in between our conversations, but throughout the passing hours, I find my body shifting closer toward you. Leg touches leg. Arm brushes arm. Eyes lock and stay locked. Fears lower and walls break down. We talk the night away, and when you drop me off later that night, we don't even kiss goodbye.

"I can't wait to see you tomorrow," you say, purely stating a fact. You speed off into the early hours of three a.m.—devil's hour.

When I wake up the next morning, it's a text from you: a four-minute-long video of you playing the violin. It's one of your favorite pieces, a French Sonata I can't pronounce the name of with lots of numbers and accents. You stand before a blue wall and close your eyes as you play. Your fingers do all the work, and you let your instincts guide you. Perfection is never your end goal, it's merely who you are. I count down the hours, minutes, and seconds until our second date.

———

JANUARY 3, 2023
　　Night

You kiss me in the car. Watching me talk until my lips go dry, I become nervous. Terrified even, I know the kiss is coming but I want it to be good enough for you. You wear a black hoodie now, your hair ruffled above your eyes as you take it out of your hood. You spent the day practicing the violin and hanging out with your friend Diana at Waffle House. You got a triple stack of pancakes with extra syrup and mounds of butter and stuffed your face full while laughing until the new moon rose into the sky. Now you fidget with your hands in the front seat of the car and watch as I trip over my words.

We're both nervous, and your voice cracks as you speak. "I like watching you talk," you confess.

"I consider myself a chronic yapper," I reply.

"So me and you are just a bunch of yappers." You giggle at such a word. "Yapper."

My body stiffens in the passenger seat, shoulders set back, fear entangled within my lips. It's a fear of not being good enough. It's a fear of you being like every man I've known before. It's a fear you won't want me after I let you kiss me.

But you pull me in quickly, and you become the exception to my fears. You drag your hand along my over-sized sweater, a crewneck with the word "Maine" engraved in navy. We kiss slowly to the sounds of violins humming from the little speaker, and as Sonic the stuffed hedgehog watches us from the backseat—how voyeuristic of Sonic—my fears of not being good enough disappear. The kiss is perfect. *You* are perfect.

"You're so beautiful," you mutter under your breath.

In between these moments, we pull away to lock eyes. You raise your eyebrows, giggling like you're on a sugar high. Your breath meets mine, and we breathe into each other's open mouths, becoming one.

"This is perfect," I mumble. "This is perfect."

———

January 4, 2023

Night

The next day we plan for the beach again. It's colder out now and there's nothing else to do in this part of Florida. Beaches are the only escape from boredom, you confess. Raining earlier in the day, the beach's sand is worn thin and the ground is cold. The sand has turned to granite. The moon is barely there, a sliver of silver at best, and the wind beats at our faces.

"I'm freezing," you say.

"Take my jacket," I reply on instinct. I've grown fond of taking care of you. The moments my fingers play with your hair. The times we sit in the car and laugh about nonsense and kiss afterward. When you tease me for being so nervous to kiss you, but then you confidently admit you were nervous, too. When your fingers are interlaced with mine and you admit you've never felt this way before. I've never felt this way either, I say back. We are both entering new, uncharted waters, both unsure of what comes next.

I think about my fantasies.

I imagine we're in the City together out at some wine bar, taking deep swigs of Chardonnay which neither of us likes, but doing so because it's cool. The walls are purple and the tables are too small for anything else besides two glasses of wine. I imagine we take a Taxi to the movies, where you'll kiss me as the projector light fades to black. Our legs wrap across each other, and skin to skin, you hold my face in the palm of your hands like you're the luckiest boy in the world. Never have I felt so loved.

You'll tell me I'm the only boy you'll ever want, and I'll say it back. Your dark hair is my moonlight and your bright, brown eyes hold the keys to my infatuation. Your nose is carved by the gods, and your demeanor is always so calm—so southern. Our comfort within each other has grown firm, and I want you for more than just a few solemn nights. I want you constantly, and our time is running out. We both know it, but neither of us acknowledges it.

We lie within the sand, staring at the stars. Never have the stars shone so bright, but now they shine only for us. I bundle you in my arms while Orion's belt watches us. "You know..." I lean forward while your head rests in the sand. "...I don't think I've ever met anyone like you before." I speak slowly, letting the wind catch my words and echo past the waves and beyond my fantasy contained in this pocket of Northern Florida.

You smile at such a confession, eyes locking with mine, incapable of looking away. I know you're capturing every moment in your mind, too, scared to let the thoughts of our goodbye enter such sacred moments. "Oh." You laugh. "You mean to tell me you've never held another guy at the beach before?"

Sarcastically, I shake my head. "I can't say that I have. This has to be a first for sure."

"Well." Every word you speak is reassurance. "I can't say I have, either."

The wind catches our laughter like it catches our words, and I wrap my arms around your head and anchor myself atop your chest like I was made to be there. I never have quite believed in love. I've never really believed in the good of boys who become men, for I've been scorned by those closest to me. But you are different. You are real, and you are kind. I wish this moment could last forever. I wish you could be mine forever. "This is a lucky first," I nudge.

You wink at me and pull me in to kiss again. In between short, quick breaths, you whisper out, "the luckiest."

I kiss you back as if I'll never kiss you again. You come back to the house later that night. White sheets engulf our desires, and we strip down until we're skin-to-skin. Your body fits into mine, and tenderly, I hold you as I touch every part of you. Your lips, which I've come to understand deeply. The inner blades of your shoulders, which shiver from the cold, but I place my hands around your body, warming you. Your chest is hairless—you shaved it a month ago to see how long the hair would take to grow back, and it still hasn't—and your legs are long. You have a tattoo of a fish on your inner right thigh, a symbol of your childhood and time in Florida. Your stomach becomes grounds for exploration, and I kiss you all over until I reach your inner thighs.

The night is perfect. Your fingers are brushing across my arm. My legs are wrapping themselves in between your legs. Your fingers are through my hair. Your lips pressing to my lips. Your fingers are across my chest, below my thighs, and finally rest along my cheek. Sand clings to our feet, which wrap around one another. You breathe out and I breathe in. We kiss as if it's forever, the white sheets eventually tossed to the floor, and our body heat keeps each other warm in the cold of a Floridian night.

Sighing out in satisfaction, we rest for the last time. Tomorrow, I leave for New York—my four days here coming to a close.

"I don't want this to end," you say.

I hold you tighter in my arms, fingers brushing across your forearm. "I never want this to end." I sigh out, breath to chest, and close my eyes. I wish to feel every ounce of your skin one last time. I wish to imagine your laughter in the front of the car as you recount the stories from your college.

You attend school in the South on a full ride, music being your saving grace from tuition. You have a crazy roommate who's always bringing boys over while you're trying to sleep. He's also gay but loves being manic, and you get into yelling matches in the middle of the night, awkwardly communicating until your roommate's date decides to leave. Violin is your passion, and instruments rule your life. You are constantly measuring life in moments like everything you know is a symphony, and I am another song in your discography.

"If only we had more time." You huff out in disappointment, clinging to my body.

I hold myself back from tears, ignoring the realization

this is the first time, at least in a very long time, another boy has been kind to me. "If only," I mutter.

Fingers wrapping around your neck, the silver chain glows in the dark. "I love your necklace, you know. I don't think I've gotten the chance to tell you that."

"Really?" You perk up, leaning forward in bed without a moment's notice. "You should have it." Your confidence consumes me whole, and I find myself lost in your voice.

"I can't." Disbelief falls over me. "It's yours."

You laugh through the dark, pulling me in for another kiss. "I want you to," you say, pulling away briefly.

"I can't—"

"Yes," you say, cutting me off. "You can. Please take it."

Self-assured, you unclip the back hook of the chain that dangles across your neck and wrap it around mine. "I want you to remember this." Your voice goes gloomy, your words rigid with the taste of bittersweet goodbye. "I want you to remember me..." Your voice trails off.

Our final words spoken break through to my closed off heart. "I want to spend these final moments holding you," I say. "Just one last time."

We lie in silence like a couple, two boyfriends who spend their final moments together. I've never had a boyfriend, nor have I been in love, but Arthur and these four days are the closest I've ever experienced to it. We hold each other as the night shifts into the morning, resting as if we'll never rest with each other ever again.

The chances of anything more than this are slim, but I dare to dream of such a world.

I spend the rest of the night holding you like my lover. I kiss you goodbye the next morning. Our time together is over, and I go numb as you leave my bed, watching you throw on your outfit from the night before, and embrace me for a hug one, final time. Our last kiss feels like goodbye, and you slowly walk out the front door towards your red car where we met only days ago for the first time.

A new truth lingers within me, and it's not sadness or anger: it's relief.

———

January 5, 2023

Afternoon

The plane ride home is marked by loneliness. Eyes set to the sky, I sit at the window seat, watching gloomy clouds overpower a tropic blue. My thoughts are clouded by you, the boy I like and may never see again.

I never believed boys like you were real. I've grown quite cynical in my desperation for love, trapped in a city where love is supposedly easy to find but impossible to hold. You are the exception.

You are real.

I don't know what would've become of our story. Perhaps we would be lovers in New York and we'd date for a very long time. We'd live together in a new apartment with brick walls and every week, we'd go out and explore the City together. Or we could've crashed and burned very quickly. Maybe we were only made to last for four days. Our kindness could've worn thin and my infatuation could've turned to boredom. I will never know what could've become of us and neither will you. Our story is complete, and now I know new truths that I did not know before.

There are good boys out there in this world, ones capable of loving and being loved. There are boys out there who are willing to hold you. There are boys out there who are willing, and wanting, to love you. Benevolence and warmth are possible, only if you're so daring to let him in. Cynicism no longer runs through my blood and relief has led to hope.

You, Arthur, are my savior.

I think I believe in love again.

10

THE TV SAYS THE MOON IS GOING TO BE RED

REEKING of alcohol wipes and poison, the boy's grandmother lays back, exhausted in her hospital bed, her eyes half open, glossed over, while a tray of tuna sandwiches sits untouched on plastic wood. Beside it, a cup full of liquid potassium and unopened chocolate pudding remains mostly full. A banana peel lies in the trash, and the sounds of hospital machines click away, taking whatever comfort which could be found and turning it into something sterile—foreign. While his grandma sleeps, the boy lies awake waiting, staring at her withering body as he forces himself to remember what she looked like before.

The doctors told the boy that his grandmother, Mimi, has lost over fourteen pounds in five days and the chance of her gaining any weight is slim. The boy talks to the doctor like a man, while the rest of the family is stuck in the snow hundreds of miles away. And despite being alone and having to watch his grandmother slowly die, the boy remains hopeful. The boy believes his grandmother has it in her, because it's his Mimi. There's no other option. She has to get better because she needs to. He *needs* her to get better.

The grandmother finally awakens. "Jake?" she mumbles.

He jumps from his chair, clambering to grab her hand. "Mimi, you're up."

She nods her head, trying to lean forward, but quickly falls back. Again, she leans forward. Her body gives out. Against her wishes, Mimi rests in a series of plush pillows that the boy brought from her home. He cannot help but notice her dried lips, cracking around the edges. Mimi prefers to be seen only when she has red lipstick smeared over her lips, a symbol of the Oscars, her favorite award show. She always wanted to feel glamorous. Red lips are glamorous.

The boy doesn't recognize his Mimi anymore.

"How are you feeling? Are you okay, um, how are you, you know I can get a nurse because maybe that would help, everyone else is stuck in the snow, but they're coming soon, I think we're gonna be okay here, Mimi because I am here with you," the boy rambles. He trips over his sentences, speaking so fast he is incapable of pausing. Fear dictates his every word, more so than he would like to admit.

"I don't—" Mimi begins to speak, puckering her lips.

"What don't you understand? What can I do to help, Mimi, I am here with you, it's going to be alright."

Mimi sighs out. "Understand."

"Oh, Mimi." The boy says her name again. It's his way of reminding himself that *this* is real. That his Mimi is actually here in the hospital room with him, and being diagnosed with a terminal disease in her early eighties is grounds for being concerned. Maybe everything will not be okay. Maybe this *is* the time. The boy pushes those thoughts away and grasps tightly to his grandmother's cold hands. Usually, they're always warm. Mimi used to joke that she wasn't warm-blooded, but "hot" blooded. She loves the cold and rarely wears jackets unless it's snowing.

Staring out at the snow outside, Mimi starts to cry. "Where are we?" Her blue eyes dart across the room, wide with fear. The clicking of the hospital machines is rhythmic, and the barren white-tiled room has become Mimi's purgatory. She clutches to the boy's hand, begging for an answer. "Where are we?" Her hand is shaking.

"We're at the hospital," the boy replies.

"Why?"

The boy chokes on her question. Why is his Mimi here? Why is he here? Two weeks ago, his Mimi was walking on the treadmill at a pace of two for an hour a day. Over three months ago, Mimi went on vacation to Florida with her best friend from childhood. Elizabeth and Mimi took over the beach, and Mimi drank a lot of margaritas. So—why *is* Mimi here now, stuck to her hospital bed, so sick he isn't sure that even if she lived, anything would ever be the same.

The boy swallows the sob buried within his throat, so guttural he can feel the grief already building at his back before his grandmother is even dead. "Everything will be alright." He speaks to her like a small child, just like the days she used to soothe him through his raged fits of anger. His Mimi would hold his hand, and slowly, while rubbing his back, would tell him that everything would be alright. At the time, he believed her.

He repeats himself again and again, rubbing his thumb over the top of Mimi's hand as she slowly drifts back to sleep. "Everything is going to be alright."

But this time, he's not even sure he believes himself. Her veins seep through her skin, and her fingers are white like unlit candles. Her fingers, dangling now with no energy to move, still have bright red press-on nails. She always bought them from the pharmacy because Mimi found them practical. "I am here with you," he coos. "It will be alright."

———

MIMI COLLECTS her stress as she rubs the boy's back. "Everything will be alright," she says. "I am here with you." The boy's grandmother is much younger now, still in her sixties, and the boy—Jake is his name—is six years old. The brother to Reed, he flails and screams while his brother celebrates his tenth birthday. Looking to rage wars, Jake screams at Reed while he tries to blow out his birthday candles—manic in his desperation to ruin the party. "Ugly cake, ugly cake, I hate you, I hate you, I hate you," Jake screams over and over again.

His Mimi holds Jake in her arms while Reed's parents try to pretend everything is fine. The boy's mother insisted to Mimi that maybe Jake's anger was from a place of jealousy. Maybe Jake needs special attention, more so than he's already given.

Mimi, therefore, was assigned the task to give Jake extra attention to prevent him from throwing fits at family gatherings. And of all the people in the boy's family, it seemed that Jake listened most to his Mimi.

"Jake." Mimi snaps, placing her finger in his face. "Behave." Her voice cuts through ice, her red nails clash against one another, and Jake goes quiet. He leans closer into the arms of his grandmother, who rubs his back through his fit of fury.

Fury. The boy was a furious child, full of anger, quick to alarm. Mimi saw herself sometimes within Jake. It was that same quickness, the ability which can make someone go from zero to a hundred in an instant, such a successful woman. But Mimi was always worried for her grandson. He was more angry than her, almost vengeful at the world. She worried that unlike her, Jake would struggle more to get better. And while she loved her other grandson, Reed, he didn't need her help. He was smart, also a trait she believed he inherited from her, so she spent more of her days focusing on Jake. He needed her help, and so she fulfilled the prophecy of what it meant to be *his* Mimi.

———

STANDING IN THE DOORWAY, Mimi cooks chicken in a red pan. The boy is older now, and after school every day, both Jake and his brother Reed take the bus to Mimi's home. Mimi shakes the dish around in the air, insisting that by doing so, she's helping the chicken cook faster. "Trust me, the shaking works." She laughs.

"Whatever you say," the boy replies. "You're always right."

The boy is quite fond of the kitchen. It's a long and narrow room, stretching from both ends of the house, and has dark wooden floors and black granite countertops. The cabinets are white and his grandma filled the walls with old paintings she found on sale, many of the paintings are of boats, while an antique clock sits in the corner of the room, just beside the dog bed for Mimi's golden doodle, Lulu. There are little pink pigs on the backsplash and books stuffed in shelves alongside the wall. While Mimi cooks, the boy now sits at the dining table, across from his brother Reed, who wears earphones to block out his existence.

He cannot help but feel lonely in these moments, and while he wishes his brother would love him more, it's not at the expense of Jake alone. The boy cannot help but critique his brother. Reed is different.

He thinks Reed might be gay, although Reed won't tell him. He understands there's nothing wrong with being gay. His Mimi always says to love everyone you don't understand, but he struggles nonetheless. How can a boy love a brother whom he cannot understand? His confusion turns to anger most days. He's cruel to Reed, so much so the boys rarely spend time together. He looks to his grandmother for guidance, confessing the stories he'd tell his brother to her instead.

The boy's grandfather sits in the living room at the other end of the house, collecting dust in a red lazy-boy chair. He flips through card decks and watches baseball most days alone, drinking in the dark. Reed confessed to Jake recently that's why Grandpa's face is always so red. "He's always wasted," Reed concluded. Jake didn't believe him and called his brother a "faggot" again. Jake learned it online and even started saying it at school. Reed doesn't talk much to Jake these days.

Mimi looks up from the stove. "Jake," she calls across the room. "Can you turn on the TV? I want to see what's on the news."

Jake grabs the remote and clicks the red button for grandma. The little TV plastered against the yellow wall in the kitchen struggles to work, and quickly, Jake flips from the baseball channel to Channel 17, the news network, for Mimi. She hates baseball. Mimi prefers Channel 17 mostly because she appreciates the cadence of the local anchor, Donna Jean Carols, an older woman like Mimi, who has a soothing voice like hot cocoa. "It's the accent," Mimi always says. "There's something so marvelous about the way her voice is so affirming yet gentle. She talks like me."

Flashing to several pictures of the moon in different stages, the little television on the wall showcases a bright, red moon set against the backdrop of New York City. The red hue hangs over the world, and from each different camera shot, the moon appears an even brighter shade of red.

"Can you turn it up?" Mimi asks. She's always been bad of hearing. Donna Jean Carols speaks directly through the TV to viewers now.

"Look out tonight for the blood moon. You don't want to miss it."

"A what?" Mimi says, still stirring the chicken in the red pan.

"A blood moon," the boy replies.

Mimi looks up from the stove, lowering her eyebrows as she squints to see the TV. Mimi is bad of seeing, too. "A what?" She blurts out "what" as if pure comedy runs in her bones. Mimi is comedic without trying to be. She's declarative when asking questions and wants to know the truth of everything happening everywhere in the world.

"The blood moon occurs rarely," Carol continues speaking. Mimi has everyone refer to the news anchor as Carol, because after all, they're best friends. Donna Jean Carol doesn't know Mimi, though. "Only when there is a total lunar eclipse. The view of the moon from the ground therefore changes appearance and will take on a red hue. During full moons, as tonight demonstrates, the red hue will illuminate across the moon's entire surface."

"Oh, golly," Mimi says, shifting her focus to her grandsons. "We have to see that."

Reed remains stoic, staring away into his phone, but Jake's face brightens at the idea. "Reed," Mimi says. No response. "Reed?" Mimi speaks out again. "Get his attention, will you?"

Jake snaps in his brother's face.

"What do you want?" Reed sighs.

The boy points towards his Mimi, smiling back at him. "We're going outside tonight to watch the blood moon."

The sun sets quickly in the Northeast, and while the

temperature drops, Mimi insists that the boys lie with her by the large tree in the front yard. It's a spot Mimi sits most days to read, peering over the rooftop of her home and past the tree line. In the distance, there's a lake, the very edge of the water shining just below the sky.

A lookout point, the house wraps itself down a heavy hill with thick trees and large, narrow bends. Mimi's dream was to always live in the woods, opposite from her childhood home in Flint. "Cold and awful," she always said, vowing to leave home at eighteen and never return. And it was true. Mimi never re-visited her childhood home, too scared of the ghosts who linger, focusing on the future of her family instead.

Living in a cottage in the woods, Mimi loves the sounds of the crickets that sing through the greenery. All bundled in blankets that Mimi carried up herself from the bottom of the hill, she falls back in a product of her own knit work. The smoke from her house sticks to the blue and begins to drift past the hills where the clouds lurk.

Behind the boys and Mimi, an old swing sways back and forth with the breeze, handmade by grandpa years before. Jake, nestled to the left of his Mimi, leans back and stares at the branches. They jut out, rusted leaves falling from the wood into piles all around him. On the other side of Mimi, Reed wallows in his teenage years, stuck to his phone, absorbed by a pair of oversized clunky headphones he got for Christmas last year. He doesn't take them off these days. He's too busy tuning Jake out.

"One Apple John Road is perfect," Mimi's words cut off Jake's thoughts. "Isn't it just a marvelous view and home. Oh, I'm just so lucky." Mimi, if anything, is idealistic. She loves her cottage and life, but especially her two grandchildren.

Reed smiles from his confines. "Yeah, it really is."

"Join the living, will ya?" Mimi pokes Reed in the shoulder and he cracks a smile. Even Mimi can get through to Reed.

Lying back again, Mimi's thick hair remains unchanged, resting like a solidified object made of spray and gel. A light blonde, her hair appears darker from all the chemicals. She shares the same hair color as Jake. Reed, gifted with the same hair as his father, is simply brunette. Mimi always wears her hair in a loosely curled bob. "Glamor," she reminds the boys. A classic shoulder length bob is glamorous. Mimi *is* glamorous.

Reaching out from the corner, the moon lurches higher into the sky. It's a full moon, still cream in complexion. Jake sighs. "Why isn't the moon red?"

"Patience," Mimi says. She's calm, quiet now, as they gather closer in their knit blankets and count down the minutes until the moon is, in fact, going to be red.

Time is slow, but Jake and Reed know not to rush it. Mimi, with a childlike curiosity, points to the sky as the cratered surface starts to change color. "It's red, it's red, it's red," Mimi screams out.

In delight, the three stare out as the moon darkens into shades of fruit punch and maroon as the night passes on. The wind is ferocious now, loud even, and Mimi scoops her boys within her arms, holding them tightly.

"It's so beautiful," Reed says. His face lights up in

awe while his body relaxes into the arms of his Mimi. His walls are down. Jake stares off into space, curious what tomorrow will bring. His jacket is tight around his collar and he loosens it, letting the cold carry him away like his Mimi. The moon continues to turn red and redder until it's finally on fire.

"Boys," Mimi interrupts. Her bright-eyed curiosity is dimmed. "There's much I want to say, but I do want to say this." The two boys tense up at such a statement. "These moments." She hesitates, carefully sifting through her vocabulary. "These moments become us. And one day, your Mimi will not be here, so it's incredibly important you enjoy every last ounce of what you have now."

"You're right, and we will," Reed finally says.

"But," Mimi puts her finger out to continue speaking. "You must act on this. Growing up is so short, and soon you'll be old. Old enough to drive, old enough to love. Old enough to become something great. To do greatness within your lives. All of this will come. But—"

"Do not forget to live in the moment," Jake chimes in.

"Precisely that, boys." Her voice wanders off past the tree line. "Precisely that.

Mimi will not die for a long time, both of the boys conclude. But still, her words hold weight. Looking past their grandmother at each other, a standoff of blue and brown eyes lock. It's a silent nod, a silent understanding of one another. It's an acceptance. When their grandmother is dead, when Mimi is no longer here, when none of this exists, all they will have is each other. And that has to count for something.

"Capture the blood moon, boys." Mimi says. "Capture it within here," she points to her chest. "And take that moment in, hold it tightly. Never let it go."

Reed and Jake close their eyes. Jake thinks of his Mimi's words. "Picture it," she says. "Love it."

And so, Jake opens his eyes and chooses to capture every single detail of the moment. His Mimi's red fingernails. Reed's brown, curly hair all tangled as he lies atop brown and gray blankets with fringed ends. Jake tastes the air, feeling the smoke run through his nostrils and down to his chest, huffing for clean air. The roofline against the trees is a clash of gray and green. The driveway is covered in red and yellowed leaves with brown tips that are easy to crumple with his fingers. The tree above them has a thick trunk with three main branches that jut off into several different split ends. The old swing his grandfather made squeaks as it sways with the wind.

Then, there's his Mimi. He looks closely at Mimi's veiny hands, capturing the way they rest against her black pajama pants. He looks at her long, blonde, curly hair she still insists on dying. It smells of chemicals and hairspray, but it's always done up in long curls that wrap around her forehead. Mimi's eyebrows are very faint now, and she draws them in with the slight touch of what must be a marker. Her eyes have a little purple around the edges, and Mimi's cheeks are always rosy. She's so beautiful, and the boy loves how his grandmother has always had her signature look—blonde hair, red nails, and black sweaters and pants. She wanted to be like Marilyn, and like Marilyn, Mimi is the Golden Age.

"Are you ready to head in?" Mimi asks the boys.

"Yeah, just one second," Jake says. Taking in another deep breath, he captures the autumn air within his hands and holds onto the moment for one extra second because he knows he will never get it back ever again, and he simply has to be okay with that.

He breathes out. "I'm ready."

———

SEVERAL HOURS PASS and Mimi is more coherent. The boy uses Mimi's iPad, her favorite invention, so she can watch the reruns of the Oscars. Jake turns on the 1974 Academy Awards, one of Mimi's favorites because of the infamous streaker. For some reason, an English teacher named Robert stripped naked and ran across the stage. Mimi cannot help but laugh every time they play the clip, and upon hearing the sounds of squealing, Mimi becomes alive with delight. "Oh, are you playing the Oscars?" Mimi asks. "Isn't that just marvelous?"

She smiles, this time with a little lip gloss on, because Mimi mustered the strength to ask a nurse for help with applying her classic makeup. While it is not her signature red, the gloss is better than nothing. Mimi is finally herself, only briefly, again.

"I know it will be alright," Mimi says. "You kept saying that earlier," she yawns again. "Everything is going to be alright."

Jake smiles while his chest heaves. "Yes, Mimi. Yes it

will." But before he turns to watch the Oscars with her, he pauses her iPad for a brief instant. Impulsivity consumes him. There's more he needs to say to his Mimi. "Do you remember—" Jake fumbles his words. "Do you remember, um, when we watched the blood moon? Back at 1 John Apple, at the top of the hill? The moon turned red. Do you remember that?"

"The blood moon?" Mimi's eyes brighten with the same curiosity from all those years before.

"I was eleven and Reed was fifteen." Jake holds Mimi's hand, desperate for her to say yes. He wishes she would jump out of bed and the two of them could run out of the hospital room together, back to where Mimi and him first saw the blood moon. But Mimi struggles to speak again, and cocks her head to the side in confusion. Her done-up shoulder length bob, her glamor, and her Golden Age beauty have now withered. Her hair now sticks to her forehead from all the sweat, despite her hands being so cold.

"I don't know," she mumbles. "I need—"

"It's okay." Jake sighs out.

"To sleep." Mimi drifts off again, incapable of holding the conversation. The boy turns the Academy Awards back on, sitting by the corner of the hospital bed, holding his grandmother's numb hand. Past the noise of a powerful orchestra and tear-streaked Oscar speeches, the noises of the hospital rattle on in the distance. His Mimi, like the wind which carries the smoke, is fading away.

"I don't want to lose you," Jake mumbles to himself over and over again. "I don't want to lose you." He weeps for the life he once had and the world he once knew. The loss of Mimi, the very idea that she will not exist, is the death of childhood. Home is gone. Safety is gone. The life the boy once knew is gone, and he must accept what's to come.

"Thank you," the boy says to his sleeping Mimi. "Thank you for being the best grandmother in the world. I'll love you forever beyond words."

———

THE TRAY in front of Mimi remains untouched, the cranberry juice in the same place as before, and the tuna sandwich, along with a half-eaten banana, slowly rots away at the bottom of a garbage can. The sounds of the hospital machines continue to click away, and the room remains foreign. There is no more chicken in the pan or Grandpa anymore. He died a long time ago, and when the boy said goodbye, he slipped Grandpa's favorite card deck into the casket. Now, Grandpa is a pile of ash atop Mimi's dresser. The boy finally accepts that this is it.

His life will never be the same, and for the rest of the days while he's alive, he will dream of when the TV said the moon was going to be red. And then, the boy will cry and wish to be a boy once again, all in the hopes he can relive all of it over again. Every memory. Every fight. Everything good, bad, and ugly, even downright disastrous. The boy would live it all again for her, just a chance to have another moment with Mimi. *His* Mimi

The boy sits by his grandmother's bedside all day and night as she sleeps, and four days later as the early onset of winter continues to bring its wrath, his Mimi passes away with the falling of snow.

Mimi's last breath takes a piece of the boy with her. The world he knows is gone. And while the boy still has his memories, even those start to slip away more and more with the passing days. *Goodbye, Mimi.*

I'll love you forever.

The End

ABOUT THE AUTHOR

Spencer Thomas is the creator of "byspencerthomas," a social media platform dedicated towards lifestyle content, LGBTQ+ inclusivity, and creative writing, with a combined following of over 260,000. Thomas is currently a junior at the NYU College of Arts and Sciences studying English on the Creative Writing Track with a minor in Journalism. He lives in New York City with his cat, Edward. To connect with Spencer, please visit www.byspencerthomas.com or @byspencerthomas across all platforms.